KINGDOM COME

....

A MILDRED BUDGE ADVENTURE

DAPHNE SIMPKINS

Quotidian Books

www.DaphneSimpkins.org

Publisher's Note: This is a work of fiction. Names, characters, places, and incidents are a product of the author's imagination. Locales and public names are sometimes used for atmospheric purposes. Any resemblance to actual people, living or dead, or to businesses, companies, events, institutions, or locales is completely coincidental.

Kingdom Come/Daphne Simpkins. -- 1st ed.
ISBN 978-1-957435-08-4

Contents

For my friends who have experienced setbacks this past year

Every day is a good day.

—Mildred Budge

DAY 1

Cause me to hear Your lovingkindness in the morning,
for in You do I trust;
Cause me to know the way in which I should walk,
for I lift up my soul to You.

Psalm 143: 8

1

JOY IN THE MORNING

God works fast. And often at night.

These were not new concepts for retired school teacher Mildred Budge, who preferred slow above all other speeds.

The full-time church lady wasn't in charge of time, however. Or even herself, when she thought about it.

Mildred had gone to bed at her preferred regular time-- nine o'clock--and awakened the next morning, smiling.

She awoke with a refreshing idea for a Sunday school lesson about those times in the Bible and in his life when Jesus most certainly smiled.

People knew Jesus wept, but Jesus also smiled.

Mildred needed a lesson for next month's Teacher's Choice day in the Berean Sunday school class, and her sister Bereans needed to be reminded that Jesus smiled because he did.

She would write that lesson for her friends: *When Jesus Smiled.*

Oh, yes.

A retired teacher, who had planned so many lessons hurriedly for fifth graders, the church lady now had the time to savor the lesson idea. She could let *When Jesus Smiled* steep through prayer and contemplation.

Breathing deeply of the hope of the day—and every day is a good day-- Mildred let the heaven-sent smile of Jesus carry her forward, blossoming in her at the pace of dawning authenticity.

Writing this Sunday school lesson was going to be a very sweet time. *Oh, yes.*

The church lady rested in that hope. *Oh, yes.*

God is good all the time. *Oh, yes.*

Gradually, with *oh yes* repeating itself inside of her, Mildred gently levered herself up, folding down the cool bedcovers as her body moved in the pace of waking prayer and unceasing gratitude.

Though she creaked a bit here and there, no aches and pains dominated her awareness. The church lady had no complaints.

And in spite of the fact that there were two other people living with her in the snug bungalow in Montgomery's garden district of Cloverdale and each one had his and her own significant growing pain problems, Mildred had slept well.

Her legs dangling over the side of the bed, she took note of her body. She was at ease. She stretched her feet toward the floor and rotated her shoulders up, then down.

Turning her head back and forth, she inhaled deeply, slowly, and exhaled in release. There was a whole day ahead of her, and she was at peace.

Hers was a seasoned peace that afforded good sleep, and good sleep created ripples of well-being and the energy she needed to navigate the day one day at a time. Every day had its own share of trouble. She didn't borrow trouble from the next day.

The day ahead was enough for her. She lived one day at a time.

A great many people in a hurry did not know this peace was possible, and the people who lived out peace could not adequately explain this dimension of being alive and also at rest. You have to experience an easeful peace to know it exists. And then you have to desire it, protect it in prayer, receive it with gratitude, and share it with others.

Almost as soon as she took inventory of her ever-growing list of blessings, Mildred heard the muffled cries of sweet Janie just down the hallway in the bedroom that had become her own and soon would be a nursery too.

Mildred Budge was Janie Fleming's guardian. Her real first name was Amanda, but Mildred still called her Janie because that is the name she used when they first met. Because Mildred had offered her home as refuge, the young woman was released early from jail in order to have her baby.

Abandoned by her lover, the mother-to-be had withdrawn, locked herself for the most part in her bedroom, and was given to fits of hard crying behind that locked bedroom door.

Janie's morning sobs were hard and relentless.

Instinctively, Mildred wanted to rise and hurry down the hallway to the troubled young woman and offer her comfort. *A warm washcloth? A cup of soothing cocoa? Encouragement and understanding?*

But Mildred had already offered that and more for previous bouts of muffled behind-closed-doors morning sickness and tears, and Janie's answer had been consistently and defiantly the same: "Leave me alone. I'm fine."

Mildred Budge accepted that there was nothing in the moment she could do for the mother-to-be except wait until the girl could let her in and allow the older woman to help her face the consequences and challenges of becoming what people called now a single mother. And an ex-con. And, without the baby's father, she was alone.

That is what Janie was experiencing. Being alone with big responsibilities coming at her too fast made her fearful and self-protective. Janie kept her bedroom door shut tight, but the truth remained.

Janie had no skills, so she had no prospects of employment.

Janie had no blood kin who were willing to take her in or even say yes to a collect phone call from jail. Her aunt in Georgia had said no when Janie called.

Mildred Budge had said yes without hesitation, "I'll pay for the call."

Janie had no one except her new friend Mildred Budge and the other ladies of the Berean Sunday school class who would not fail Janie Fleming if she could believe that; but abandoned by the father of Little Mister and her hormones in a pregnant uproar, she could not.

As far as Mildred knew, Janie had never experienced a long-term trustworthy relationship, and so she did not know how to believe it when one was offered.

Thinking about Janie's situation, Mildred felt her breathing speed up and become shallow. Her shoulders tensed as she listed Janie's problems. All of them were serious, and all of them would need to be solved. Knowing the problems, Mildred still did not have the immediate answers.

"God is good all the time," the church lady proclaimed before her feet hit the floor, and the encroaching worry retreated, though it did not fade away completely.

The church lady continued to preach to herself. "Thy kingdom come. Thy will be done. Oh, yes."

Mildred breathed deep draughts of gratitude as she stood upright, lengthening her spine while patting her short brown curls into some kind of arrangement.

Donning her white chenille robe from where she had laid it across the top of the honey-colored wooden hope chest at the foot of her bed, Mildred tread softly down the hallway and checked on seven-year-old Chase asleep in the bed in his room now, her former study. Then, she placed her hand on the door of Janie's bedroom and eavesdropped.

The crying had quietened. Perhaps the girl would sleep some now.

Passing through the small kitchen at the back of the house and a cup of steaming black coffee in hand, Mildred tip-toed her way toward the sun porch at the back of the bungalow off the kitchen. It was the only personal space left to Mildred Budge in her own house. It was where she read her Bible, prayed, and when she had a few minutes, wrote down the words for Sunday school lessons and devotionals that always hummed inside of her.

Espying the still dark house of the Deerborns across the back field, Mildred tipped her pink stoneware coffee mug in their direction before taking a first sip, remembered her waking idea about the Teacher's Choice Sunday school lesson, and seeing Jesus smile in her heart, Mildred smiled, too.

For the lesson, she would begin by describing the light in Jesus's eyes when he smiled. Instantly, she could see that light! When smiling, Jesus's eyes crinkled at the corners against sun-burnished skin, and the light of his love for others made the exact color of Jesus's eyes irrelevant, though if she were to try and describe it, she would say his eyes were the color of love's light. His smiling eyes reassured people afraid of judgement and condemnation, *that's not why I am here.*

She would show them a dozen places in the Bible where Jesus's kind eyes were shining, and they would see that love light, too. And when they did—her heart leapt up at the thought!-- they would be overtaken with holy joy. *Oh, yes.*

In that moment, the momentum of Jesus smiling happened again. Joy coursed through Mildred Budge and became the experience of that promised abundant life.

She whispered one of her favorite morning sunrise prayers: "I declare every cell of my body to align with the perfect will of a lit-up smiling trustworthy love of my big Brother Jesus. *Oh, yes.*"

She gave herself to the prayer, feeling the energy work its healing heat throughout her from head to toe. *Joy. Joy. Joy.* The message of joy repeated itself like an undercurrent of living water inside of her. She breathed the truth. The gospel is real. The gospel is true. The gospel is life-changing, and the astonishing fact was that the joy of a smiling Jesus could happen to anyone.

Mildred Budge woke up with joy every day, and it was real.

2

SUNRISE, OH YES

The second cup of coffee was no less good than the first. That had always been the case for Mildred Budge whose parents and grandparents had been coffee drinkers.

The change in her morning coffee routine was that the retired school teacher had adjusted now to not driving through morning rush-hour traffic to the grammar school where she had worked for twenty-five years. She no longer drank or even wanted a third cup of coffee. The early morning caffeine helped her wake up until it was too much, and then the next sip of a third cup made her jittery. Once you have experienced at-ease peace, you don't like any kind of jitters.

The church lady opened her Bible and placed her hands on the words underneath her searching fingertips. The Bible was unlike any other book you could read. It would read you right back if you let it.

But the Bible could do even more than that. Just holding the Bible settled her. Focused her. Sated her thirst for living waters just like Jesus promised that dear lady at the well when he asked her for a drink. *Did Jesus smile at the woman at the well?*

Mildred closed her eyes and considered that moment in time that had never stopped existing. That thirsty woman was always there by the well, or someone like her. Jesus was always there by the well to greet her, or someone like her. The promises were real. People who drink my living water don't get thirsty. *Oh, yes. Jesus smiled.*

Mildred Budge inhaled deeply of the promises that abided within her. Steady, deep, slowed, at-ease breathing continued. Prayers that existed as a humming inside of her all the time, erupted to the surface, becoming utterances of hope and gratitude.

In a rhythm of speech that could easily have become a song, Mildred said, "Word of my heart. Joy of all creation. Thy kingdom come, thy will be done. Change me all you want, oh, yes," she asked, as she heard Chase rouse down the hallway.

Mildred's awareness tracked the soft footfall of the small boy's journey toward her, and she felt the magnetizing pull of the child's attention searching for her as she listened for him.

"Out here, my boy!" she called in her raspy morning voice.

She felt Chase stop and change direction. Turning, turning, the child repented of the wrong direction, and followed the sound of her beckoning voice, appearing almost as an apparition in the doorway between the kitchen and the back sun porch, waiting silently for her to bear the responsibility of starting a conversation.

Twisting in her chair, Mildred positioned herself to really look at the skinny seven-year-old kid, all rumpled and boyish, barefoot, his sandy-colored hair going this way and that.

"Top of the morning to you, Chase," she said. Her voice broke slightly. It did that in the mornings and, sometimes now, when she was leading the singing with Anne Henry in the Berean Sunday school class. It was a great disappointment to hear her voice break at inconvenient times, for Mildred Budge had grown up using her voice publicly to teach and pray and sing and be a helpful member of the church. To hear her voice break filled her with disappointment that others might suspect that her testimony had a crack in it.

The little boy stared at his guardian expressionless, his hands hanging limply at his sides, his bare feet gripping the hard red brick of the one-step threshold separating the kitchen from the sun porch. Her born-again inner Miss Budge prayed silently, 'Let the whole world be overtaken with a holy joy. Start with this boy today,' she breathed exultantly. Her heart pounded with hope in her chest. She loved him so.

But what she said to the little boy staring blankly at her was, "It is a cool morning. Better put on the new sweatshirt over that T-shirt, and I will stir up a bowl of yummy oatmeal just for you."

Chase hesitated, thinking. Then, still wordless, Chase turned and went back to his room. He wasn't unhappy. He wasn't angry. He wasn't backward or brain-damaged in any way. He didn't need counseling or medication. He just wasn't a talker. There were words in the little boy, but they did not come out very often. He had lived deep, deep inside himself for a long, long time. Like a deep-sea diver, the boy was slowly making his way to the open air above and other people. Fran. Winston. Jake. Sam. Belle. Steev. And occasionally, Janie, but she mostly ignored him.

"The dark blue sweatshirt," Miss Budge suggested, calling after him, her voice strengthening with use, as her inner Miss Budge prayed, '*Give him words and the Word. Oh, yes.*'

The suggested blue sweatshirt was brand new, and the only-washed-once fleece inside would still be soft against the skin. *So cozy!* She wanted Chase to feel safe and warm.

Thinking warmly about the light in Jesus's eyes and the lesson she would write later for her sister Bereans, Mildred left her blank notepad and open Bible and went humming to the kitchen to prepare the boy's breakfast.

Chase always woke up hungry, and that made her happy. Mildred Budge loved to feed people.

Chase returned and sat down at the table, picking up his spoon. He had not combed his hair. He had not brushed his teeth. And he had put on a green and blue plaid flannel hand-me-down shirt donated to him by a mother of five who wanted to help Mildred and her boy after he had been dropped off at her doorstep, abandoned by his young frustrated parents who couldn't handle him and had given up trying.

Mildred smiled at the boy's daytime ensemble. She did not call his choice of a flannel shirt instead of the new blue sweatshirt disobedience. Little boys often had their own thoughts and while pursuing them did not always hear what you said. Many people of all ages were hard of hearing in all kinds of ways.

Mildred sat down next to Chase and fought the urge to ruffle his hair and feel the outline of his head in her hands. She had that impulse from time to time with many people. Her banker. The butcher at Publix. Sam Deerborn next door. Steev the preacher who lived across the street and even Jake Diamond from time to time when he came to call and seemed concentrated on some task at hand, his pulsing thoughts behind squinting dark eyes beckoning her piano playing fingertips that responded to heads as if they were different kinds of instruments which needed to be touched and tuned by a church lady who loved the gospel and music.

"Chase, do you want a banana?" she asked. She stifled a cough that also came in the morning and more often now inconveniently during the church service these days as well.

Coughing too much at church caused heads to turn; sharp looks occurred. Pariahs coughed in church. She had been training herself not to cough during church, but often failed.

Without looking up, Chase nodded. His hand gripped the spoon in a hard clench, his flesh pink at his finger joints from the intensity of his grip. He held his fork the same way. And a pencil. Though he had had no formal schooling to speak of, the boy could read and write though his penmanship was almost indecipherable.

Learning that about Chase had surprised the retired teacher. She did not know how the boy had learned, for when she met him he had been a truant of sorts—not going to school and not home-schooled either. The computer in his room had been his daytime friend.

His parents had deemed him slow, a social failure, a helpless case that they could not solve and kept him home. He had lived very deeply inside of himself, the way Sam, her neighbor who had dementia, did now.

A lot of people lived deeply inside themselves in varying degrees and for many different reasons. All kinds of labels existed to point them out. Sam had dementia. Chase was just a little boy growing up with parents who didn't seem to know how to handle their responsibilities. Their son was slowly coming to the surface.

"And so am I," she breathed softly, a confession that was also a declaration and a prophecy. She was learning how to budge every day, and she wasn't finished praying. She never was.

The boy was beginning to surface, was gaining weight, and sometimes, he almost smiled. He was coming along. Janie would come out of that room one day. Little Mister would arrive. Life could not be stopped. Everyone was growing up in their own ways at the pace declared by the Master Timekeeper of Eternity and Maker of sheep in his pasture.

"Help his parents find their way, too, wherever they are," Mildred whispered, as she peeled the banana and sliced it over his bowl. "And help me help the boy."

Her serving hand stopped just that quickly. Sometimes too much help doesn't help after all.

Instantly, Mildred decided not to add the cinnamon, the brown sugar, or the raisins to the bowl of steaming oatmeal. The boy could see the oatmeal toppings on the table in front of him. Every day that passed he was getting better at seeing what was in front of him and helping himself. That was an important lesson to learn. He needed to see them. He needed to want them. He needed to spoon his own sugar, add his own raisins, experience the explosion of flavor that is cinnamon, and decide for himself whether he liked it or didn't.

She stopped herself from adding more to his bowl. Instead, she left the goodies on the table for Chase to see and choose for himself. One day, after time had passed and he had grown to trust her love and the table set before him, he could arrange his own feast just by asking, like the other brother in the story about that prodigal son was urged to do.

But that morning, Chase settled down in front of his cereal, his head bent over the cereal bowl.

She smiled and gave in to the impulse to ruffle his hair after all.

What a sweet head the boy had.

Just barely, Chase tilted his body toward her and leaned his head against the warmth of her expansive waist for more affection.

The Sunday school lesson about Jesus smiling still brimming inside of her, Mildred Budge closed her eyes and prayed for holy joy to overtake him.

3

BREAKFASTIME

Chase stood up, holding the now empty cereal bowl with two hands. After blinking rapidly twice, he registered the echo of Miss Budge's directions of what to do next—though he had heard it many times before-- and took the sticky bowl and spoon to the sink and set them down. Standing on tip-toe, Chase reached the faucet handle and turned it on.

"Well done," she approved heartily. "It is time to comb your hair and brush your teeth. Don't worry too much about brushing those teeth in the back. No one sees those teeth unless you smile or laugh."

Chase stared at her, digesting her directions seriously at first. And then he saw her smiling, and he fought a smile, covering his mouth with one curled fist. His eyes grew less dark and almost twinkled. Not quite—but almost!

Joy was coming!

"I need to write down some words," she confided. The confession became a request. "I need just a few minutes in that chair in the sun porch. I won't be long."

She did not ask, 'Can you be alone for just a little while and trust that I will be here?' but that is what she meant.

Chase didn't answer her as he shuffled off back down the hallway to brush a couple of his teeth and comb some of his hair. His narrow shoulders were gently sloping, and she felt his size and vulnerability. Soon, she must schedule a visit with a dentist and see how his teeth were actually doing. She would need to find a dentist for children. The task was added to her mental to-do list. The woman from church who had given him that shirt would know. *What was her name?* The answer would come later, and Mildred had learned not to panic at the slowness of recall.

Choosing a new steno pad from the wooden magazine rack now serving as her temporary writing desk in the sunroom, Mildred sat down again on the cushioned wicker chair. She resumed staring out at the back field and the Deerborns' house. They weren't up and about yet.

"What was I thinking about?" she mused.

She didn't immediately remember that either. It had felt important though. And the idea had made her happy. *What had she been thinking about?*

She didn't remember.

Time passed. Her attention drifted. She thought of her mother. Her father. Chase going to school soon. Janie's lack of a high school diploma. Her own graduation from high school. Then, college. Her parents' graduation gift of the hope chest and how she had filled it once upon a time the way young women do at that romantic stage in their life when they have completed a milestone of their youth and are thinking about what will be next.

Like other young graduates, Mildred had begun to fill her hope chest with homemaking items. Deluxe guest bath hand towels. Pillowcases embroidered with butterflies. And for a while, Mrs. Budge's daughter had added potholders she had made herself with a small red metal loom and bags of multi-colored fabric loops. She had loved making them in small patterns that could have been a square in a homemade quilt. But they were potholders.

Before the chest overflowed with these, her mother had gently steered Mildred to look harder at the future. *You love to read. You could become a teacher or a librarian.* Mildred went back to college and got certified to teach. And as time passed, Mildred began to give away the items in her hope chest to girls getting married.

Then, the newly certified public-school teacher began to refill that honey-colored hope chest with practical items: flannel night gowns, pajamas, and deluxe quilted robes in pastels and matching Daniel Green slippers that women of a certain age keep on hand for when they are in the hospital and need to look presentable should the preacher come to visit and pray for her recovery.

A little boy brushing some of his teeth grew older while Mrs. Budge's daughter ruminated.

A young pregnant woman locked up in her bedroom stopped crying; and though her face was wet with tears, she finally fell asleep.

Planets orbited.

Stars burned out.

Subatomic particles played a game that confounded physicists: whichaway?

Across the back field that connected the two neighbors' yards, the light in the Deerborns' kitchen flickered on. It was one of those long-lasting bulbs that had to warm up before it achieved its fullest potential.

Her long-time neighbor Belle opened her back door and settled a stuffed white plastic bag of kitchen trash on her back stoop until she was ready to walk it all the way to the trashcan around on the side of the house.

Her husband Sam used to take the trash to the big outside can, but he didn't now. Sam didn't remember anymore. Belle still set the morning trash bag there, just like she always had as if Sam would be again one day who he had been once upon a time. But Sam walked right past the trash bags these days, going on his wanderings.

Later, Belle would see the bag, accept the implications of its presence one more time, and wrestle the bulging white plastic bag to the trashcan herself.

"Lady Fran is here," Chase announced suddenly, pointing behind him to the front door.

"Lady Fran is here?" Mildred confirmed, using the boy's name for her best friend. "I didn't hear her knock. Fran didn't knock, did she?"

Chase shrugged, turning away. He had combed his light brown hair with water and plastered it into place. She detected the fragrance of minty toothpaste.

"Frannie doesn't knock," Mildred muttered to herself, rising slowly, her steno pad almost slipping off her lap. Her right hand grabbed the pad, and she stuffed it hurriedly in the side pocket of the wooden magazine stand. "I didn't expect Fran this early in the morning."

Mildred blinked fast, thinking. Fran was back from her honeymoon early, and Mildred had thought her best friend would have chores like laundry and going through the mail that she needed to do before coming over for a visit. Mildred mused aloud to herself, "I think Fran is early. Or is it later than I think?"

Before Mildred Budge could answer her own question, the newly married Fran Applewhite Holmes came around the side of the house and charged up the two back steps to the porch's door. She was wearing her light blue denim pants outfit with red gingham trim on the cuffs of her pants and the collar of her jacket. Her white Keds looked new. But they weren't. Fran kept her Keds clean with a little *Spic and Span*. She poured some of the soap granules on a paper plate, added a drizzle of water, and created her own shoe-cleaning paste and rubbed that paste on her white canvas Keds.

"Chase told me you were here. I was just coming to the front door," Mildred explained.

"You didn't hear Winston's truck, and I was afraid to make too much noise because I didn't want to wake up Little Mister's mother," Fran announced.

She stamped her feet and stepped through, looking around as if for the first time. But it wasn't. Fran had been coming in through Mildred's back door for years.

"Did I forget you were coming this early?" Mildred asked, settling back into the white wicker chair.

"You couldn't have forgotten. I didn't know I was coming until a few minutes ago," Fran replied tartly, letting the creaking screen door hit her in the behind to muffle the sound of it closing. No slammed doors for Fran Applewhite Holmes who was always early everywhere she went and called it being right on time. When other people appeared within a minute or two of their appointment time, she greeted them politely, but deep-down Fran considered them tardy.

"I am forgetting something," Mildred said. And that was the truth. Something else was bothering her now. She was forgetting something more.

"We all are," Fran said dismissively. "Don't worry about it."

Mildred brushed aside the concern and said, not for the first time, "I woke up in a good mood, and I wanted to write something down before I forgot it."

"You always wake up in a good mood," Fran declared.

Her comment didn't sound like a compliment, but it wasn't a criticism either. It was just a statement.

"Where is Chase? I have brought him a present. Winston picked it out. We found a model car kit in the hotel gift shop."

Her best friend was talking too fast.

Mildred stopped and turned. "What's wrong?" she asked pointedly.

"What could be wrong?" Fran asked, dismissively. "We brought the boy a present," she said, placing it on the kitchen counter.

Fran turned her back on Mildred and faced the door that led to the kitchen. "Is the girl up yet?"

Mildred shook her head though Fran could not see the movement.

"What were you doing out here?" Fran asked, avoiding Mildred's question by asking one of her own.

"I was beginning to write a Sunday school lesson. Just got started."

"Why don't you give up teaching Sunday school and let someone else take a turn? You've got a full house. You've put in your time. Retire from Sunday school teaching, too.

Look at me. I don't have any responsibilities on Sunday mornings anymore. The secret to being as happy as I am is to get a life of your own."

Fran's voice was too loud for the room, too bright for so early in the morning.

Fran Applewhite Holmes wasn't happy, and she was trying to sound like she was.

Mildred's eyes widened, her mouth opened slightly in a surprised 'oh," and Mildred left human time immediately. Fran's question sent Mildred Budge instantly into kingdom-come time. There, Mildred was not offended by the judgment in her friend's question. Instead, she knew incontrovertibly that the only reason Fran would say something as harsh and as untrue as she just had was because she was not herself. Her best friend had come home early from her honeymoon. Something was wrong, but Fran wasn't ready to talk about it.

"I will get dressed," Mildred said, moving toward her bedroom where she had laid out her outfit for the day the night before.

"I am going to do something about your kitchen," Fran declared.

"Make me a piece of toast, will you?" Mildred asked. "And a glass of Ovaltine."

Mildred didn't hear Fran's answer, but when she returned a few minutes later, dressed, hair combed and her face washed, a dry slice of toast was on a paper napkin on the table. No butter. No jelly. And it was cold.

4

WHILE I WAS GONE

"So what has been happening while I've been gone?" Fran asked. She was leaning against the sink, one foot crossed at the ankle in front of the other—her characteristic 'I can't sit still right now' stance.

"Janie stays in her room, but Chase is coming out more. Jake ordered some kind of special playhouse kit and had it delivered here. It is their project. The big box is over there in the middle between those trees," Mildred said, pointing with the hand that held the dry toast. "Jake has had Chase— and Sam, too—involved in putting it together."

Fran pivoted and squinted. "I don't see it," Fran said, peering in that direction through the sun porch window.

"The bigger pieces are still in flat boxes on the ground. I think it is like some kind of Lego kit, only it is a playhouse. But you know Jake. He likes to do things the right way. He said something about laying the foundation. They haven't gotten very far yet. Jake said they are waiting on two solar panels for the roof."

"Solar panels," Fran repeated, and then shook her head. "Are you going to mind having a kid's playhouse in your back field?" Fran asked. "The boy may not be living here for always. Then, what will you do with a playhouse?"

The blunt question stabbed Mildred right in the heart. She couldn't think about losing the boy. She willed herself to be calm and to sound that way.

"Jake needs to do something to help him adjust to retirement. He managed the buildings and grounds of the whole university for a long time. He needs something to take care of now. They have also been working on that old car at the other house," Mildred explained, going to the fridge. She poured herself a juice glass size of milk and added two tablespoons of Ovaltine.

"You still drink that?" Fran said. "I forget they even make Ovaltine."

"They make it," Mildred said. She drank Ovaltine when she didn't have time for a fuller breakfast.

Fran changed the subject abruptly, watching Mildred drain the small cup of Ovaltine. She walked over and took the cup from Mildred and placed it in the sink.

"You about ready to get a move-on?"

"Where are we going?" Mildred asked, though she knew the answer. She was stalling while she thought about what she had been planning to do that day. Go to the new house and tag furniture to move to their booths. Clean out the previous owner's desk. Shred five years of his income tax documents that no one was worried about but her. She had bought the house lock, stock, and barrel, and that included an old car in the garage which she had planned to have towed off, but Jake had told her to keep it. *The boy and I are going to work on it. Chase likes to work with his hands. And he can think—really think.*

24

Before Mildred could say anything, Fran said, "We really need to go see our booths. It has been two weeks since we checked on our inventory."

"We should do that," Mildred agreed, though she would rather go back into the sun porch and write down some words before they disappeared altogether.

"That model car kit Winston picked out for Chase runs on double-A batteries. I forgot to buy batteries," Fran confessed, surprised by her own oversight.

Mildred opened her junk drawer. She had C, D, and AA batteries on hand.

Fran looked over her shoulder. "Might need triple A."

Mildred reached into the back of the junk drawer and her fingers found a package of those, too.

"When are you going to clean out that drawer? It is a mess in there."

"I will get around to it one of these years," Mildred said.

Janie's door opened quietly. They heard her padding down the hallway to the kitchen. She was surprised to see them.

"You are still here," Janie announced, drawing back. Her thin brown hair was stringy. Her flannel pajama bottoms and a man's white T-shirt were baggy and unwashed. She was barefoot and moving heavily, clumsily. "I thought you had gone to the other house."

"She lives here," Fran replied tartly, taking in the girl's slovenly appearance.

It didn't matter that Janie was pregnant. It was no excuse. Fran did not like seeing able-bodied people sleep past the time of day when the real work of building a good life begins.

Janie turned and went back to her room and quietly closed the door.

Fran snorted slightly. "Does she ever come out and stay?"

"Only when she thinks I am not here. I find myself trying to stay gone when I am running an errand or working at the other house so Janie can have some time to roam around and find something to eat. She needs to wash her clothes," Mildred added thoughtfully. In that moment, she couldn't remember when Janie had done her own laundry last. Mildred only knew that she had not.

"That is just what I wanted to hear," Fran said, clapping her hands. The sound was jarring, and Mildred eyed her friend. Something was off. Fran was trying to sound like her old self, but she was doing a poor imitation of it.

"Let's do Little Mister's mother a favor. Let's go check on our inventory at The Emporium," Fran said. "You need to get out of this house."

Fran's voice was feverish with an intensity.

"We have a life to live. Let's go live it," Fran said, her voice sounding louder than it needed to be.

Eyeing her best friend, Mildred wondered what had happened on her honeymoon.

"You get Chase," Fran said.

"I am forgetting something," Mildred confessed suddenly. It was nagging at her.

"Oh, you were trying to write something, and you can't remember what that was. It will come to you. Don't worry about it. When you worry about it, you simply take longer to think of what it was. Let's go."

Mildred shook her head uncertainly. "I am almost positive I am supposed to be remembering something."

"Don't go the way of Sam, Mildred Budge. We have talked about that. We are going to keep our wits."

Mildred nodded solemnly. "Let's do that," she agreed, pushing aside the worrisome thought. Whatever she thought she was forgetting would come to her eventually. It usually did.

"I will see if Belle would keep an eye on Chase," Mildred offered. "Jake is coming over in a few minutes to pick up Chase and take him over to the rental house. They are going to change the oil in the old car. Chase can stay with Belle until Jake gets here."

Fran nodded, her body growing more tense from standing still. She needed to be in motion. "I see Belle out in her yard. I will just take Chase over there. Come on, Chase. Auntie Belle would like a good visit this morning, and then Uncle Jake is going to come and get you later."

Chase came out of his room solemnly. He was wearing shoes. He eyed them both quizzically.

"Don't you want to go visit with Uncle Sam and Auntie Belle?" Fran asked, leaning down to meet his eyes.

He took a step back and stared at his feet.

"Come on," she urged. "No need to be shy. We know everybody. We are going this way," she directed firmly.

Chase followed Fran silently through the kitchen, down the step to the sun porch and out the back door through the field to the Deerborns' house while Mildred brushed all of her teeth and combed her hair some more. She wasn't having a good hair day.

Mildred tapped on the closed bedroom door and told Janie, "We are leaving," but the self-imprisoned inmate did not answer her.

5

THE PRESENT MOMENT

Fran pushed the speed limit on the way to The Emporium, an old department store that had been converted into a vendor warehouse where local entrepreneurs recycled merchandise. Mildred and Fran rented two booths to sell household goods which they hunted and gathered from estate sales mostly, though recently Mildred's purchase of a second rental house fully furnished was proving a gold mine of recyclable goods.

Fran scooted through two yellow traffic lights, stifling a curse when someone cut her off at a turn. The stifled muttering surprised Mildred.

"I don't know what gets into people these days," Fran said, exasperated. But it wasn't other people who were driving aggressively. It was the newlywed Mrs. Holmes.

Fran didn't sound like a woman who had just come back from a relaxing honeymoon. Mildred tried to suppress that concern by staring out the window at the landscape flashing by. Montgomery was a blur of old houses and rambling yards decked with yard art. She passed Porky Pig, frogs holding umbrellas, and her favorite, Humpty Dumpy sitting precariously on a brick garden wall. Where there was no art, there were often flags hanging from poles. Sometimes, they were American flags; but just as often now, they were college football flags. There were a lot of Auburn, Alabama, Alabama State, and Tennessee fans who lived in Montgomery.

Parking in their usual place six spaces down from the front door, Fran hopped out, landing solidly with both Keds-clad feet on the grimy warm asphalt, scuffing the soles and toes of both shoes. She didn't stop to take notice.

"We are burning daylight," Fran called out to Mildred who was lowering herself more sedately from a seat that was higher than her own in the red and black Mini-Cooper which she had offered to drive, but Fran had not heard her.

"I am coming as fast as I can," Mildred explained, but Fran didn't hear that either.

Without a confirmation glance behind her, Fran strode across the parking lot and pushed open the main door, frowning at Streeter who had not propped the front door open invitingly as it should have been.

Before Fran could ask a question that would have put the old man on the defensive, Streeter greeted her and her business partner loudly, leaning on the newspaper spread out on his counter, getting newsprint all over both forearms.

"Good morning, Mrs. Holmes. Miss Millie," he said. "I figured it was about time for you two gals to show up."

"We are here now," Mildred announced, something in Streeter's tone causing her to grow concerned.

He read her mind and smiled reassuringly. "You two girls have done a good little business lately. You will see soon enough," he predicted, looking back down at the obits. Streeter read them every day, and was always able to discuss the lives and times of the recently deceased and about to be buried and their grieving kinfolk.

"Thanks for the heads up," Fran said with a farewell wave as she turned the corner down the aisle that led to their booth.

She didn't want to spend time making chit-chat with Streeter about dead people. Life was for the living.

Mildred smiled consolingly at Streeter, glancing at his open newspaper and glad when the phone rang. He reached for it, giving her an out to hurry after her business partner.

Mildred caught up with Fran at their booth, ignoring the overflowing booths on either side of the aisle that were crammed with second-hand merchandise. She had to make herself go past the glass jewelry booth that famously touted glass bead necklaces and clip on earrings, the kind Kathleen used to wear.

Mildred missed Kathleen and still thought about her big red glass earrings that one of her daughters had inherited, no doubt. In the back of her mind, Mildred was keeping an eye out for a pair of red glass earrings like them. Mildred loved costume jewelry, though she rarely wore the pieces she owned. She was still thinking about having her ears pierced and buying small diamond studs, but hadn't quite made up her mind if she wanted the burden of keeping up with something that was both so small and so valuable.

Fran was standing in the middle of their booth space, which was half empty.

"We are wasting floor space and burning money because if we are not selling goods we are paying for empty booth space," Fran sighed, a failure. "What with the wedding and the honeymoon...."

"And Jane and the baby and Chase...." Mildred interjected, shouldering some of the blame.

"You are doing more than your share," Fran said bluntly. "And that new house you bought has or will be a godsend if we will just take the time to line up the items we need to bring over. Winston is sitting on ready. And I am ready," Fran declared, and her loud voice was jarring.

"I just had to fall in love, didn't I?" Fran moaned more to herself than to her best friend who did not respond.

Hands on her hips, Fran pivoted slowly, surveying their booth. "It is what it is," Fran said, taking stock. "What's happened is our business has gotten away from us is what has happened. And it shouldn't have happened. It is not who we are." Fran considered their problem. "We ought to have some things in the back storeroom we can bring out."

She was dismayed by the challenge of trying to carry heavier items.

"We need Winston for the bigger pieces. He is kind of busy today," she said, and her attention drifted momentarily as she thought of him and then through will alone, it returned. She declared, her voice aggrieved, "I wish I were taller and stronger."

And as soon as Fran Applewhite Holmes said those words, Mark Gardiner appeared at the end of the aisle, and walking quickly beside him was Liz Luckie, the serial widow and the renter of the overflowing booth beside theirs.

Wearing a navy blazer that had a grey silk handkerchief in the breast pocket, the tall, strong man wasn't dressed for hard work or heavy lifting.

His current girlfriend and the widow of four dead husbands, Liz Luckie was dressed more for a cocktail party than a stroll through The Emporium. She was wearing her signature look—a midnight sheath of a dress with three strings of layered white pearls. There was a diamond accent clasp and matching earrings. Liz was dressed for an evening out, and the time was mid-morning. People were still going to Hardee's for a breakfast biscuit.

"Do you remember the Spiegel catalog?" Fran asked Mildred quietly as Liz approached, holding Mark's arm as they walked down the aisle toward them.

There was a posed quality to Liz's appearance that could have easily fit inside the glossy pages of the Spiegel catalogue.

"I think so," Mildred admitted. She was reluctant to say more, but she actually remembered that glossy catalogue very well. Once upon a time she had spent hours paging through the glamourous pictures of outfits and sparkling jewelry that you were supposed to need and want as you grew older. There was even a season when she had selected items for a trousseau to be stored in her hope chest.

Her mother had found the catalogue and seen the dog-eared pages, treating her daughter's ensemble choices with a kind of reverent soberness. A pillbox fur hat. A hand muff to match. Wool skirts and slacks in winter plaids of red and blue and green and gold. Deluxe oxblood leather loafers with tassels and classy gold initials of the designer. Two winter coats. One in camel with big brown buttons and the other a rich ocean blue double-breasted rain coat with a wide lapel, the kind that a spy might wear who was on a mission for the CIA. The catalog had stayed in the magazine rack by the fireplace while Mrs. Budge digested the implications of her daughter's selection and taste. Shortly afterwards, Mildred's mother opened the lid of her daughter's hope chest and suggested that Mildred begin to give away the potholders and pillowcases and restock it with items she would use. That is when Mildred had begun to buy the quilted housecoats and Daniel Green slippers you wore indoors but could walk out to the mailbox in without hurting them. Then, her mother had handed her a college catalogue and talked about Mildred having a goal. That is when she told her, "You could become a teacher or a librarian." The moment returned, bittersweet as good advice often can be.

Seeing Liz in what could be a Chanel little black dress, Mildred felt the smarting sensation of window shopping but never really buying anything from that catalogue though she remembered it with a fondness that was later replaced with cruise ship brochures and the pictures of fancy dining room meals and exotic ports of call. Yes, she had enjoyed that season of page-turning the Spiegel catalog. Now, Mrs. Budge's daughter dreamed of a cruise.

"When those two are together, they remind me of a couple of models from that catalog," Fran said.

Mildred nodded quietly, feeling the comforting presence and guidance of her down-to-earth mother who whispered in her ear straight from heaven. "All of that passes away. Only love remains."

"I preferred J. C. Penney myself," Fran said, plucking at the collar of her denim ensemble. That is when she saw that her clean white Keds were grimy.

"Girls," Liz said, greeting them too brightly. "We meet again." Her voice was frosty friendly.

Mark nodded his hello, looking quickly past them down the aisle for something more interesting than the two of them.

"We are making the rounds," Liz explained, stepping into her booth and patting the white pillow sham on the twin bed. It was lacy. Dusty, too. Liz fluffed her hair at the back of her neck and scratched with one long mauve painted fingernail. She fixed a smile on her face and turned back to them and noted the emptiness of their booth.

"Business is great," Fran boasted, her eyes glinting. "As you can see," she said, waving triumphantly to the empty floor space that seconds before she had been bemoaning.

"Aren't you supposed to be on your honeymoon?" Liz asked abruptly.

Liz's question hung in the air—taunting Fran.

"I am right where I am supposed to be," Fran rebutted firmly. "Isn't this the same merchandise that has always been here in your booth?"

Liz shrugged an artless shoulder, her chin going up. Liz wore heavy make-up and had not blended it along her jawline. The distinct difference in the applied color from Merle Norman and the natural tint of her skin created the effect of a mask.

"Mark and I are running errands," Liz said, repeating herself and ignoring Fran's pointed question. "We stopped in here on a lark. We are thinking about putting some of Mark's furniture here. He is planning to downsize." Liz studied her overpacked floor space. "But it is just not going to work," she said, surveying the crammed booth. "His furniture is so big we could only showcase one or two pieces at a time. And furniture that big! I don't think there's a market for it anymore. It would take forever to sell. And we don't have forever," she sighed.

"I am putting my house on the market," Mark declared definitively, moving closer to Liz. He was a handsome man by any standard. He could move furniture easily from the back storage area to their booth if either Fran or Mildred would coax him to do that, but neither woman even considered it.

Mark was dating Liz, and you don't ask another woman's romantic friend to help you tote furniture. He might misunderstand, and neither Fran nor Mildred wanted to be misunderstood.

Still, Mark was eye-catching. He had a good head of hair that grew darker and then greyer sometimes. No one knew who his colorist was. Still, whether his hair was greying at the temples more than usual or not, Mark was always dressed for being in public. And his skin was a healthy copper tone from working outdoors in the vintage plant business. That is how he and Mildred had met. Mark had brokered some vintage plants from the backyard of the old Garvin house which Mildred now owned and was renting to Steev, the new preacher.

"There's the work of bringing in the furniture and moving it out....." Liz's voice trailed off. "It is all so tedious. So tedious," she lamented, and she began to wring her hands—a move that neither Mildred nor Fran had seen in a sister church lady in a long, long time.

It gave them both pause. Liz was anxious about something, a display of vulnerability that they had not seen in her before.

"We will think of another way, Elizabeth," Mark soothed. "The main thing is to keep the main thing the main thing."

"Oh, you are so right. You just don't know how right you are!" Liz replied feverishly.

"I have just about made up my mind to let my booth go. Life is meant to be lived, and I don't want to spend my days here among these relics of the past." And then Liz Luckie said something no vendor at The Emporium had ever said in the entire history of the business, "I don't like antiques. They're so old."

Hovering near Liz, Mark spoke up, his voice as warm and ingratiating as a self-conscious TV reporter who aspired to become an anchor. "You two girls wouldn't want to take over Baby's lease?" Mark suggested promptly. "She doesn't have time for this."

"She doesn't have time for this," Fran repeated, studying the man in front of her.

Feeling her attention, which was familiar to him, Mark smiled becomingly, and said persuasively, "The extra floor space would let you spread out some, and you two have always seemed to me like the kind of gals who want to spread out wherever you are," he said.

Fran's gaze narrowed. Opportunity was knocking, and Fran believed that when it did, you opened the door.

"If you are serious, Liz," Fran interjected, directing her response to the vendor who had signed the contract. "Millie and I might take over your lease, but it would need to happen today. Right now. No thinking about it. No changing your mind later. Today, while it is today, we will take it," Fran offered Liz on the spot.

Mildred's mouth went dry.

Mark raised one imperious plucked eyebrow and then leaned down and whispered in Liz's ear.

Liz covered her mouth, stifling a giggle. "Mark says...." She began and then thought better of it. "If you want to spread out, why don't you two girls consider everything in my booth a gift to you just to get out from under it? I don't want to have to fool with moving everything out. It is too much! It is just too much! I am learning how to let go and let God," Liz explained airily.

"And keep the main thing the main thing. Some things, like time and being together, are worth far more than money," Mark said, his dark eyes glowing warmly. "Are we good to go?" he asked Fran directly. He didn't look at Mildred.

"Good to go," Fran agreed readily.

"Well, then if we are good to go, let's go," Mark announced with a quick bark of a laugh.

Liz laughed too, looking up. She enjoyed standing next to him. She was the kind of woman who needed to see herself in the eyes of a man who liked women, and Mark liked women.

Mark brushed the part of his hair with one hand, checking that it was in place, and then concluded the deal with authority. "If there is something to sign, let us know."

The use of the word *us* told the whole story of the main thing between them and shut out Mildred and Fran immediately. It was Mark and Liz now who were an *us*, and the couple on the verge of falling in love lived in the center of the universe where all other life forms rotated around them.

"Oh, there will be something to sign," Fran assured him firmly. "Streeter will make it work," she said with confidence. "He doesn't let any grass grow under his feet."

But Mark and Liz didn't appear to hear Fran's commentary.

"We are going on then. We are leaving the past behind as of this very second. Good-bye, Yesterday. Hello, Today. It is just us now keeping the main thing the main thing," Liz promised Mark, looking up.

He had never looked taller or more posed to be seen.

Liz looped her hand through his arm, and Mildred saw him pat it possessively.

Turning one last time, Liz said, "I am going to tell that grumpy old codger at the front the plan du jour."

"Be sweet," Fran advised, her body growing taut with controlled action. She was ready to move, but she was waiting for them to leave.

When the two lovers were almost at the end of the aisle and close enough to tell Streeter what they wanted to do about the booth, Fran finally said, "I guess there's more than one way to skin a cat."

"I have never understood why anyone would want to skin a cat," Mildred replied automatically. And then she thought about what she had said, and added, with a kind of wonder in her voice, "Until today."

6

TIME CAPSULE

Fran got busy in their now extended booth immediately.

"Mildred, grab that end and help me shift this girly bed over here. Some mama sending her baby girl off to college might want this bed for a college dorm room."

It was a white twin bed with gold trim. Very French Rococo. "I am just surprised it doesn't have a canopy," Fran said.

"A dust collector. Do people vacuum a canopy?" Mildred asked.

"No. They wash it like they do curtains," Fran said, though she had never done that or known anyone who had. Fran often had definite answers to questions not relevant to her personal history.

"We are going to move this lamp over here. And scoot this tiny rocking chair over here against our end table. The upholstery is cross-stitched. Some people like that, but they need to be able to see it," Fran said, repositioning the throw pillow so passersby could read the stitched Bible verse: *This is the day that the Lord hath made. Rejoice and be glad in it.*

Fran worked while she talked, and pretty quickly they had thinned out Liz's over-packed booth and made their own floorspace look better stocked.

"That will do until we can get Winston over here to shift some of our other bigger stuff from the back loading dock here. Yes. That will do until later," Fran said with satisfaction.

Both hands on her hips again, Fran nodded decisively, pleased with herself and the situation. She was working. Progress was happening.

"You ready to skedaddle?" Fran asked Mildred suddenly.

That exit prompt was new. Fran had been using it for a couple of months ever since Winston had told her there are three ways a cowboy leaves a room. 'He hightails it, he moseys, or he skedaddles.'

"More than ready," Mildred said at the pace of moseying.

"Let's check in with the man," Fran said, looping her purse over her arm. "You need the loo before we go?"

Mildred shook her head.

"Then what are you waiting on?" Fran asked, impatiently.

Her early morning tense mood was back just that quick, and Mildred didn't know why.

They walked the long aisle back to the front counter. Mildred stole a quick glance at another jewelry counter where old-fashioned costume glass jewelry was sometimes on display. No red glass earrings today. Mildred didn't exactly shop for something she only half-way wanted. She kept an eye out for it though.

Streeter was on the phone and smiled when the two women approached, holding up his right forefinger to signal, *I'll just be a minute. Hold on.* He was nodding to the speaker on the other end of the phone.

"We might. But I don't know. I can't go shop for you. I am supposed to stay here at the front counter. Yes. Yes. I could write that down. And yes, if I see what you are looking for I could call you, but I can't shop for it for you. I know. I know. I know," he said, shrugging at Fran who was grinning. "We ought to think about having a personal shopper for people who call in. But right now, we don't. Okay. My pleasure," Streeter said, hanging up the phone.

"What do they want?" Fran asked. "They seemed to really want it."

"A lot of people call here wanting me to check for an item of merchandise so they don't have to come here. By the time I covered three floors and looked at every booth, I would have forgotten what I was looking for. That is probably what would happen," Streeter predicted. "That caller wanted gold cuff links."

"Gold cuff links," Fran repeated, turning. "I saw a pair in that cabinet down there on the left. Booth 46. Second shelf. Monogrammed though with an S or a dollar sign. I didn't stop long enough to study it. I didn't see the price."

"Do you want me to go look?" Mildred offered.

Neither of them answered Mildred so she turned and went back down the aisle to booth 46.

As Mildred walked away, she heard Streeter say, "I hear you two gals are taking over Lady Luck's booth."

"We are," Fran confirmed. She crooked one elbow on the countertop near Streeter's open newspaper and signaled for him to come closer.

Had it been anyone else, Streeter would have held back and muttered something about personal space. But it was Fran Applewhite, and Streeter liked her. She was a go-getter; and although he had slowed down over time, the manager of The Emporium still thought of himself as a go-getter, too.

Streeter leaned in, both arms resting on the counter, smudging the glass countertop with the newspaper ink on his arms. He didn't care. There was a bottle of Windex sitting on the floor right underneath the cash register and a roll of paper towels. He cleaned that glass top counter two or three times a day. He liked the way the cleaned glass looked afterwards, and he liked the way Windex smelled: fresh.

"Streeter, old buddy, old pal..." Fran began playfully.

"Who says I am old?" Streeter challenged, his eyes brimming with amusement.

"I meant best. Best buddy. Best pal," Fran amended quickly, her blue eyes shining with a teasing purpose.

"I'm listening," Streeter assured Fran, leaning toward her.

"Is there a discount on the rent when the two booths are side by side?" she asked, winsomely.

His eyes warmed. Streeter wasn't afraid of flirting or negotiating. "If there isn't, there should be," he said. "One vendor. Less recordkeeping. And if the vendors are you two hard working ladies who pay attention, there should be a financial incentive to keep you happy and selling stuff here at The Emporium where the future meets the present while honoring the past. That's the new motto. What do you think?"

"I love it, and my business partner and I are very happy here where the future meets the present while honoring the past," she said, repeating Streeter's motto.

He grinned easily, his eyes brimming with intelligence and amusement. He liked negotiating a deal with Fran.

"Oh, I'm happy. Aren't we happy, Millie?" Fran asked, as she felt Mildred return.

"I am very happy," Mildred agreed, though she was hungry. She was ready to go find some lunch. "Those cuff links are monogrammed with an S, and they are thirty-five dollars. If that helps."

"It does help," Streeter said, nodding appreciatively. "I will call them back ere long," he said eyeing the phone. But he wouldn't call them immediately. He couldn't afford to let a telephone shopper think that this was the best way to find something. Customers needed to come in and browse.

"I am just back from my honeymoon," Fran said.

"I heard you got married. Lucky fellow."

"Aren't you sweet?" she cooed, sweetly.

"Not too many people think that," Streeter said immediately, his gaze darkening as he remembered. "That woman who was just here. The Luckie woman. Boy. She told me what was what, and said they were headed to that casino in Wetumpka for lunch. That pretty man with her said that she had won ten thousand dollars at that casino a while back. She acted like she was about to go do that again. Do you think lightning is going to strike twice?"

"They used to have her picture on that billboard over by the interstate, the exit near the hospital. It said she was a winner, and you could be a winner, too."

"Was that her? I used to see that billboard and wonder if she was real."

Fran nodded. Mildred sighed.

"Liz has also buried four husbands. They all had life insurance."

Streeter digested that information, looking out the door through which Liz and Mark had exited. They would be halfway to the casino in Wetumpka by now.

"With that kind of money in the bank, what's she doing with a booth here?

"She was bored, Streeter. Just bored."

"Our vendors work to earn money to send kids to college and whatnot. There's a lot of whatnot going around," Streeter said.

"She won't be coming back if we can take over her booth," Fran said.

"Ten thousand dollars," Streeter repeated, his head shaking. "What I wouldn't do with ten thousand dollars."

"You can't know it from looking at our booth as it was— it is better now—but Mildred and I have a great deal of inventory to bring over; and as soon as I can talk my sweet husband into loading his truck and bringing it over here, we are going to take full advantage of our additional floorspace. We have a lot of inventory to move. Don't we, Mildred?"

Mildred nodded. Her stomach growled loudly and inconveniently. She took two steps back, away from Streeter and Fran.

Streeter looked past Fran down the aisle where the two booths were located side by side. "You do have one of the best locations on the first floor. It is right on the way to the bathrooms and the Coke machine."

"And we appreciate that," Fran said, following Streeter's gaze to the end of the aisle.

He looked down at her hand resting lightly, gently on top of his, and then he grinned, settling into the rhythm of Fran's end game. "You are wondering about a discount for the two booths on the first floor. But you are not asking about your other booth downstairs because I can't give you a discount on that booth."

Fran turned, as if suddenly remembering the basement booth. "We would like to let that downstairs booth go as soon as we can find a subletter or..." she appeared to consider the options. "Or, we will work out the length of our contract and be happy with the two booths on the first floor, which is easier for us to restock. You can see the landscape better when the booths are combined. We have limited manpower," she admitted. "Not that I am complaining."

"Nope. No, you two ladies never complain," Streeter remarked, looking at Fran and then at Mildred.

"There's nothing to complain about at The Emporium!" Fran announced brightly. "Do you have any complaints, Millie?"

Mildred wanted a bacon biscuit and an icy cup of orange juice. Glancing at the clock, Mildred saw they had under twenty minutes to get to the fast-food place before they switched over to the lunch menu altogether. Any remaining biscuit now would probably be cold and dry. The bacon would be charred and brittle. They kept the cooked food under a heat lamp, but that was just for show.

"I have got no complaints," Mildred assured Streeter, agreeing with Fran.

"So, what I am hearing you say is that you want those two side-by-side booths on this first level because you are taking over that Luckie woman's booth, but you would like to let go of the basement booth when your contract runs out. Or, if someone would like to sublet it before then, you would be open to letting it go early."

"You would be in a position to hear about someone wanting to sublet it. Maybe the person with the booth on the other side of us in the basement? Maybe that person would like to stretch out a bit," Fran suggested.

Streeter scratched his chin, finding a random whisker he had missed in his morning shave. He tugged at it thoughtfully. "I think I know who has that downstairs booth beside yours. I would have to look it up to be sure. Everyone is always asking for more space. Everyone. All the time. We have a waiting list for booths," he said, playing that last card at the last moment.

"Would it be too much trouble?" Fran asked sweetly.

And that is when Streeter broke into a big smile. "Nothing is too much trouble for you, Miss Fran." And remembering Mildred, he added gallantly, "Not you either, Miz Bulge."

Mildred didn't correct him. Fran was doing business. Besides, a lot of people got her last name wrong.

"Aren't you the sweetest thing?" Fran replied, placing her hand on the open page of his newspaper. "You are reading the obits," she observed.

"Every day. We bring nothing into this world, and we can take nothing out," Streeter opined, more to himself than to a vendor of recycled goods who obtained much of her inventory from the estates of people who couldn't take it with them.

"I usually know somebody or the relatives of the somebody who has passed on. I like to keep up with the news in case their kinfolks come in here. I like to be able to express my condolences. But there's more in the newspaper, too. I read the sports page to see whose children are getting scholarships. I like to be able to say something to people when their children get their names in the newspaper. Everybody loves for you to know who their children are."

And that is when Fran's eyes filled instantly with tears. "People do love that," she agreed. "We must make an effort to keep up with people and the people they love."

"That is what I think," Streeter agreed, nodding his head vigorously. "I heard about you getting married. I didn't see it in the newspaper. They used to print the pictures and names of the girls getting married, but they don't do it anymore. And they should. Just publishing sports and obits is not right. It doesn't tell all the best stories. I see bankruptcy stories and arrests and murders. But they don't make a habit of publishing the best going-forward-in-life stories.

"Why, not so long ago, in Saturday's edition, they published the titles of the sermons the preachers were going to give the next day and the hours of service. They don't print that good news anymore either. If I didn't know for a fact that newspapers are as good as dead—they just haven't published their own obits yet—I would think about starting a newspaper, and I would publish all the news that is right to print: church times and the sermon topics, the bride's picture and the date she says I do, and I would...." Streeter faltered as he began to offer his vision for a better world, a better Montgomery.

"What?" Fran asked, curious. Fran stopped thinking about booths and business then. She stopped and considered the man in front of her.

"I would publish more letters to the editor, and I would think about naming the editor. People still write letters, but they might just as well address their letter to Mr. Anonymous, because you don't know who picks the letters and why some letter gets picked and published and others don't."

"Have you ever written a letter to the editor?" Fran asked, instantly curious.

Streeter thought about denying it, but you don't look into the piercing blue eyes of Fran Applewhite Holmes and not tell the truth.

"I have things on my mind, and I have written a few letters. I've always signed my own name. I will tell you that. If you are going to say something, be willing to sign your honest-to-God name, I always say."

Neither Fran nor Mildred asked if his letters had been published. They both subscribed to the local morning newspaper, but the letters to the editor were only published on Sunday mornings. They were always too busy to read the Letters to the Editor on Sunday mornings because they were trying to get ready for church. The trash collectors came on Monday so they threw the previous day's newspaper away without reading the letters. They didn't say anything in the moment, but each woman knew and decided to check for Streeter's name on Sunday mornings in the Letters to the Editor section from then on. It is only right to keep up with people and what they had on their minds. Streeter was right about that.

Feeling suddenly that he had said too much, Streeter stood taller and flipped the page of the newspaper to the classified ads. After they left, he would start from the beginning again. When customers were in the store and close to checking out or stopping by to talk, he appeared to be reading the newspaper all day long.

But on slow days he fished out his *New York Times* Crossword puzzle book and went after those big words with thirteen letters or so. He liked the words not many people said anymore. They made him feel at home in a world that was hightailing it. "I tell you what I am going to do," Streeter announced deliberately. "I think I know someone who would like that downstairs booth."

Streeter did not like to use the word basement very often. He preferred the word downstairs. It had more romance. At The Emporium, a romance with the past drove sales all day long.

Fran stood back now, patient, her negotiating instincts reigned in so that Streeter could make a decision that was fair to The Emporium and good for two reliable vendors.

"I'm going to discount the rent on the first-floor second booth 25%. That's what I am going to do."

"That's very good of you," Mildred interjected sincerely. She had been weighed down by the extra booth, and now they were lightening the load considerably. He might be able to find a subletter for the basement booth.

"That would be really wonderful, Streeter," Fran said. "We thank you."

Streeter eyed Fran, forgetting Mildred. "They should have put your wedding picture in the newspaper. You are a beautiful woman, Mrs. Holmes, and you can tell Mr. Holmes, I said so. If I were running that newspaper, that is what I would do. I would publish your picture first thing. I may have to write them a letter about this whole idea," Streeter said, thinking out loud. "No one has brought up honoring the brides and marriage lately. Some married people still love each other," he said. "Quite a few if you are paying attention to the survivors in the obits."

The phone rang then just as the bell over the front door also rang, signaling new customers were coming in the front door.

"Good morning!" Streeter called out briskly to the customers, while he glanced at the phone and shook his head. "The recorder can get that," he explained.

"No need. Please answer it. I think we're agreed. Are we settled?" Fran said.

"I am settled," Streeter assured her, reaching for the telephone.

Fran stepped away, closer to Mildred. "Will you call us when you want us to sign any kind of paper?"

"Emporium," Streeter said into the phone. "Hang on a minute will you?" he asked the caller.

Placing a palm over the receiver, he assured Fran, "The paper to sign will be ready over there under the cash register the next time you girls come in. Just ask whoever is here and sign it. Read it first, you hear me," he advised with a quick wag of his forefinger—a gesture many people made when they wanted to tell someone else to do something, firmly.

"Twenty-five percent off the second booth," Streeter affirmed, one hand cupped over the receiver. "And we will find someone for downstairs asap."

Fran didn't leave. She waited for him to answer the caller's questions, and then, when he had completed the call, she sealed the deal. "Done and done," Fran agreed happily. She was herself again—standing there, thinking, planning, negotiating with a businessman.

"You girls go get a good lunch to celebrate—the wedding and all," he encouraged. "You have got to stop and smell those roses!" he added-- the man who wrote letters to the editor.

In the moment, the manager of The Emporium looked past the two women out the front door and let himself absorb the motion of people outside the sprawling time capsule where he worked. They were neighbors and strangers, passersby, going this way and that, in a hurry, lost, finding their way, growing older all of them.

A companionable stillness came upon them. Streeter lingered in the moment with Fran and Mildred. There was a calming pace to their farewell.

Mildred saw Streeter inhale deeply, taking in the moment. If they had asked him to come along, he would have left it all—just gotten in the truck with Mildred and Fran and driven off with them to Chappy's for an early lunch. They would have sat at one of the booths in the far-right corner away from the restrooms and the kitchen, and they would have talked about Montgomery and how it had grown and what needed to happen for the public schools and the teachers and how the hurricane season would start soon. They would have traded the list of what they deemed emergency items they had in their respective closets, items bought to be ready for trouble. And each one would have made a comment or a suggestion about how to become better prepared. Buy these gloves. Don't forget to grab your prescriptions. You might need a manual can opener if the power goes out. How much bottled water is enough?

Maybe they would talk business too—what was selling, and what wasn't. Did anyone say the name Scarlet O'Hara anymore? Streeter would know.

Streeter came to himself all of a sudden, blinking as if the bright sunlight filtering in through the front window was suddenly too bright. This time when his eyes met first Fran's, then Mildred's, there was a searching quality. He was looking for something—a quest he didn't admit to or share with anyone most of the time.

"You gonna have a good day, Streeter?" Fran inquired kindly. It sounded like a question, but it was really encouragement; and in a way that good neighbors know, it is truly a kind of prayer.

The old man grinned, and when he did, both women could see the boy in him, the young man, too. His honest-as-the-day-is-long eyes shone. His gaze warmed with affection and good will. Reaching out, he took Fran's hand, the one wearing the diamond engagement ring and the gold wedding band. Streeter looked like he was going to kiss the back of Fran's hand in an old-fashioned gesture that only happened on television now.

Mildred watched, and she could feel something pass between them. She almost knew what it was.

"My day has already gotten better by just seeing you," Streeter said, blushing slightly, his hand moving to the

54

safety of his newspaper page as soon as he let go of Fran's hand.

"You sweet old thing!" Fran said gaily. Then, looking more like herself and sounding like it, too, Fran asked her question. "Streeter, if we see a letter in the newspaper that sounds like you, what name will be signed at the end?"

"Funny you should ask, because people don't ask."

Fran waited.

"Thomas S. Jefferson," he said. "When I was born my parents had high hopes for me. High hopes."

When they looked around the time capsule called The Emporium, it was not an oval office or a fancy corporate building. It was a meeting place where people traded second-hand goods and called some of them antiques.

Fran nodded succinctly. "That name would look good in print."

"My parents must have thought so," he agreed, as the phone rang again. This time he didn't reach for the phone. Instead, he watched as Fran turned and led her business partner out through the front door toward Winston's truck, which had grown hot in the mid-morning sun.

Thomas S. Jefferson watched as Fran stopped and lifted her face to the sun, and when she felt its warmth, he grinned to himself, because in beholding her, Streeter could feel it too—and the warmth from the morning sun felt so good.

7

STAYCATION

Fran walked more slowly toward the truck than she had toward the building when they had arrived an hour and a half ago. At one point right before opening the driver's door, the sound of an airplane overhead snagged Fran's attention. She looked up.

Overhead an airplane passed by. It wasn't the small crop duster plane that you could see from time to time when you drove across the bridge over the Alabama River. It was a big airplane headed to Maxwell Air Force Base.

Both Fran and Mildred often saw planes coming and going from that direction, but neither woman liked to think about the implications of why so much military air traffic was necessary.

When the plane was out of sight, Fran asked, "Do you think we will ever go anywhere really?"

"Right now, we are going to go find some lunch. Let's go get something to eat," Mildred replied, climbing up and into the truck, her purse resting momentarily on her lap before she would shift it to the floorboard that needed to be vacuumed.

Fran switched on the air conditioner immediately and left the window slightly cracked to blow out the warm air.

She didn't shift the gear into drive immediately. Instead, she gave The Emporium and Streeter one last look.

Mildred followed Fran's gaze. They watched Streeter push open the front door of The Emporium, and wedge the doorstop to hold it open, letting the air conditioning out but the fresh air and the sunshine into the place where he spent his days among the romantic relics of the past and with the people who revered them.

"What an extraordinary man he is," Fran remarked. "Extraordinary. Do you see?"

For a moment, Mildred's best friend was lost in her admiration of Streeter, guardian of the time capsule called The Emporium.

"Did you see?" Fran repeated her question, and her eyes glowed with admiration.

"I saw," Mildred replied.

"You saw," Fran affirmed with satisfaction. She cranked the engine and looked behind her to see if it was safe to back out. "I think we are too late for a biscuit."

Mildred checked the time on the bank clock across the street. "Do you really want to go out? How about a peanut butter sandwich at the new house? We could tag furniture for Winston. We could eat our sandwiches by the swimming pool with our feet up and have one of those staycations they talk about on the evening news when they report that no one can afford to go anywhere these days because of the price of gas."

"Is the bread fresh?" Fran asked. "I have standards."

"Mostly," Mildred said. "I bought a loaf of bread three days ago and left it there with the peanut butter and some bologna in the fridge."

Since she had bought the new rental house and was cleaning it out, Mildred had been stealing staycation time away from her own house there, exulting in the quiet rooms and the quick lunches and snacks that didn't require much effort or any conversation.

"That's fresh enough," Fran agreed.

A shadow crossed Fran's face, and she concentrated on her driving, steering them out onto the street headed in the direction toward Mildred's new rental house and the furniture she would either keep or sell in their booths.

"Are you thinking we should have talked about Liz's booth before I said we would take it?"

That had occurred to Mildred, but she had been so relieved that Fran seemed suddenly recharged, she didn't care. Mildred told her best friend the real truth.

"Right now, what I am thinking is that I don't want to go to my own home. Though I originally planned to rent the new house out, I don't seem to be in a hurry. Sometimes, I think I bought the house as an escape. I think they call it a man cave."

"A woman cave," Fran replied easily.

"Have you ever heard me say that before? I do not want to go to my own house," Mildred confessed.

Fran deftly steered Winston's truck over to the curb and slowed it down, shifting to Park. She let the motor idle gently, keeping the air conditioner running but in no hurry to drive on.

"I don't want to go home either. Can you imagine either one of us saying those words before today? But I am not surprised to hear you say them."

Mildred turned to face her friend. "I am surprised to hear you say them."

Mildred braced herself to hear some story about Winston and the cut-short honeymoon. She could see each one of them retreating to their respective homes and resuming dating, bidding one another good-night. Wearing wedding rings, they might go back to their respective homes and resume the easier path of dating again, meeting for meals and watching TV before retiring apart.

Fran leaned her head back against the head rest and exhaled the words she had been holding back—the reason she didn't want to go home, where she would have to live out the reality of what she was about to confess. "I found a lump, Mildred. A lump."

Fran closed her eyes as if remembering the moment when her honeymoon had become the event—*I found a lump*. "Maybe the lump will be nothing, and we can start over. Did you hear me say those words out loud? I have been thinking those words, but I haven't said them out loud before. How did they sound?"

Mildred slumped slightly forward, clearing her throat before she spoke. "I heard them. I hear you," Mildred assured her.

Staring straight ahead, Fran asked her best friend, "Do you ever get tired of giving yourself a pep talk?"

Behind them a car with a loud muffler approached, so loud that it felt like the sound would rock their car as it drew up beside them and idled, slowing down as it reach the four-way stop.

Both women waited for him to make his turn and take the obnoxious muffler away with him before speaking. As the noise retreated, Fran said, "I bet he snores."

"I wouldn't want to live with someone who snores as loudly as that," Mildred said, tentatively. She was giving Fran a starting point to tell her more.

"Winston doesn't snore. I knew it already. Before we ever got married, we would have supper and start watching TV together, and my sweet Winston would fall asleep in his recliner and not snore. Sometimes when he fell asleep, I muted the TV and read the subtitles and watched an episode of *Law & Order* like that, and I enjoyed it. It made me happy that he was resting and that I could sit there and be happy, too, letting him sleep and reading the subtitles."

Mildred kept silent. Fran was finally talking. She needed to talk.

"And, I wondered after we found a lump if Winston was relieved in a way because he looks tired sometimes when you catch him off guard. I am kind of energetic all the time, and Winston is more easy going. He is a light sleeper during the night and a napper during the daytime. And I wondered if he would not mind me having a lump for a while because then I would become more tired for a little while, and he could get some rest. That thought scared me," Fran said, her gaze stark with remembering. "It was the first time I have thought something like that. That he might not know it yet, but he might find out when I am too tired to be a go-getter that he liked me better tired. I push. I know I push. I know I have pushed you sometimes to do the things I want to do like starting our business at The Emporium."

Mildred could not deny that, so she didn't. But she didn't regret being pushed by Fran either. "We are doing all right," Mildred said. "You and I. We know Streeter because of The Emporium, and he is extraordinary."

Fran nodded matter of factly, the wonder of Streeter fading with the romance of the past. "I like Streeter. I know who he is, and I like him."

"I like that about you, too," Mildred offered because she could feel more coming, and she wanted to postpone the inevitable sadness that she felt rising up. She stared out through the window.

"Can you imagine that I thought Winston might like me to be tired? That's strange, isn't it?" Then more to herself than to Mildred, Fran said, shaking her head over her own confession, "He is not like that. Winston is not like that at all, but that is what fear can cause you to imagine."

Mildred could not answer Fran.

"Winston gets tired. He gets tired more than I do. But he is not like that."

"We all get tired after a while."

"Knowing you are tired can hit you all of a sudden. Then, you feel weak from the realization. And when you feel weak, you can get scared. Fear is worse than cancer, don't you think?"

"Oh, yes," Mildred said. "Fear is worse than cancer."

Her response was a different version of a pep talk.

"You and I understand what tired means, what cancer is, and how to face trouble," Mildred assured her.

Fran stifled a wan smile. "Of course, everything will be all right. I know that. You know that. But I thought there would be more time not to have to say those words to

ourselves or each other for a while. You know? I thought--
and I am old enough to know better-- that I would be able
to enjoy my honeymoon without having to add worry to it.
I thought there could just be a little spell of being at ease,
just a little while of holding hands with a loose grip and
watching the sunset. The water was pretty down there,
Millie, and when the sun set, it was glorious.

"If Streeter owned a newspaper, he would publish a
picture of the previous sunset every day. Imagine having
an ongoing record of one sunset after another. It had been
a while since I had taken the time to look, Millie. Really
look. But you know, Mildred, since I found the lump,
everywhere I look the view is spectacular now. That is what
a lump makes happen. And so there's that, isn't there?"

"The silver lining of that," Mildred agreed, and the pep
talk made her tired.

In that moment, Mildred followed the trajectory of
Fran's gaze. She was looking at a pile of dead leaves in the
street drain on the corner. It needed to be cleaned out.

Fran continued. "While we were in The Emporium, I
forgot about the lump and self-pep talks and knowing that
Winston likes to take naps. It felt so good to forget to worry.
I got caught up not thinking about the lump, and it felt so
good that I just couldn't shut myself up. That's why I took
Liz's booth without asking you. And because taking it
meant that this lump-thing will be nothing. I believed it
right then. I want to believe it now. But I am old enough to
know better, Millie. I am old enough to know this lump-
thing will probably be something that will make me tired
and worry all my friends. I don't want my friends to worry

about me. I am a go-getter. That's who I am. It is who I have always been."

Mildred focused. Inhaled. Moaned inside: *thy will be done, thy kingdom come.* The words were a buoy in an ocean of fear. You could hold onto them and know you were safe. You might not be able to see the rescue ship, but you knew it was coming. The church lady dwelt in those words.

Fran took a deep breath. "I just wanted to believe that we had all the time in the world. Like we could just say *yes* when opportunity knocked, and it seemed to be knocking, and I didn't want to think this lump-thing could happen to me. It has happened to other women. And now it has happened to me. And I thought I was too old for it to happen to me. I don't even think about myself as being too old for anything. I have never thought I was too old for anything. Did you know that?"

"I can see how you have never thought of yourself as too old. I can see that," Mildred said.

"But when we found the lump, that is what I thought. I thought I am too old to have breast cancer. It is going to have to be something else. It will be a calcium deposit."

"It could still be that," Mildred suggested.

"But it is not," Fran replied. She sounded tired—not a go-getter at all.

"Winston wouldn't wait. He made me call the mammogram place from down there, and they wouldn't book an appointment without a doctor requesting it, so Winston made me call my doctor, and my doctor called the mammogram place. They called me back and promised to work me in. They worked me in—gave me an appointment fast. That is why we came home early, and we didn't talk about it because I just didn't want to talk about it.

"Last week I was in love and on my honeymoon, and this week I am home with a lump-thing, and I don't want to go home now," Fran said.

"They did an ultrasound after the mammogram the very afternoon we came back. It is something else, and when she told me, she said, 'I'm sorry.' And they scheduled the biopsy."

"The biopsy," Mildred repeated. She had not yet said the words lump-thing, and now they were saying biopsy.

"We are staying at Winston's house right now. We go back and forth. I thought we would decide which house to keep and which to sell, but first, falling in love distracted us, and now this lump-thing business has put that decision on hold."

"You will figure it out," Mildred encouraged.

"I figured Winston needs to be in his own home if he is going to go through this with me. And then I thought if this lump business turns out to be something worse, he wouldn't want to have sold his house and be living in mine. Wouldn't he be awfully homesick to be living in my house and me not there and his house gone? So, there we are," Fran said finally. "Here we are."

"We are all right," Mildred assured her. "We will figure it out. You will see."

"A few minutes ago that old man named Streeter fought the impulse to kiss my hand. I saw that. Did you see that?" Fran asked without looking to Mildred for confirmation.

"And I wasn't too old for that, and just because he felt like that for a second or two, I fell a little bit in love with Streeter while also so very much in love with Winston and the sunlight and the way the heat feels on your back when you just walk across an asphalt parking lot even though it's hot, but it still feels good, and the breeze comes and you mentioned a biscuit, and I thought I could eat a biscuit or something because I am hungry, which isn't like me, but I am hungry—hungry for so much, Mildred!-- and now I have this new idea I have never had before that I am too old. Too old. Me?"

"Are we old?" Mildred asked quietly. "Are we old, really? Who says?"

"I say," Fran declared. "Today, I am too old to have a lump, but I have got one anyway. Today, maybe we made a mistake about Liz's booth. Maybe I made a mistake. You were just an innocent bystander. If things don't go our way, I will be tired for a good long while. The work of filling the booths will fall on you and Winston. And Winston gets tired. And you just bought that new rental house, and I love cleaning it out. Don't you? I love choosing the pieces to go first to The Emporium and tagging them with a price and knowing that in a week or two, change will happen, and we will need to send some more items over there. I really like to work. Are you tired, Mildred?"

"I wasn't tired this morning when I woke up," Mildred said, staring out through the passenger window. It felt to her that she had awakened on top of the world, and now she wasn't. She didn't want to go home; but if she did, she would have liked to crawl into bed with a good book and read for hours. Mrs. Budge's daughter hadn't done that since she was a kid home from school in the summertime and let herself read from morning till night.

"If we had asked Streeter to come with us, he would have flipped the store's sign to CLOSED, locked the front door, and walked out with us. I knew that, and it made me forget for a moment."

"Streeter wanted to come with us," Mildred agreed readily, and she did not marvel that she knew that about him. You can know a lot about other people if you take the time to see them. When you do, they can turn out to be extraordinary. Even Liz and Mark, probably.

"Trouble comes, but it doesn't stay. That has been one of our mottoes. We will get through this," Fran declared.

But her voice had a strange new quality to it. Fran Applewhite Holmes didn't believe her own pep talk.

Mildred made herself ask the question that needed to be answered. "When is the biopsy?"

"Tomorrow, early." And then with an air of resignation that Mildred had never heard before, Fran said in a strange version of a pep talk, "I can't wait."

8

LUNCH TIME

"Jake is here," Fran said, her voice growing distant. She parked in the street near the mailbox. "Jake didn't know we were coming here, did he?"

"We didn't know we were coming here," Mildred said.

Fran reached for her purse, but she did not open her door. She sat in the truck hesitating, not wanting to go inside. "Do you know how many times I sat with families during their season of hospice care?" Fran asked suddenly.

Mildred's purse was on the floor. She left it there and listened. "You have talked about what it was like from time to time, but I never counted how many times you have done that."

"They would call me right at the end, usually after midnight—always late. I always knew that call was coming and laid out an outfit so I could get there in a hurry, though people don't die at the end as fast as you think. It is not like on TV. I would drive over in the dark, and the streets are different at night. There are street lights sometimes, but mainly it is the moon which keeps you company. And it is always cold in the car no matter what the season. The car inside feels cold and empty. When I got there, I would park right out in front by the curb-- not in the driveway," she said with a rueful smile, "So people could come and go."

"Someone would usually be watching for me and open the front door as if they thought I was going to come in and all of a sudden have an answer or an antidote or know something they didn't know about how to stop death." Fran twisted in the seat and faced her best friend. "I have seen a lot of people die, and I don't know anything. Not a thing."

"It is hard," Mildred murmured.

"Yes. It is hard. It was always hard. Sometimes, they needed someone to be in the kitchen making a snack or some coffee. Sometimes, they needed me to answer the telephone. It would start ringing because somehow people would know, or they were waiting to hear an update and would finally call and have to ask. Whatever the family needed, that is what I did.

"Eventually, I ended up in the sickroom—I hate that name for a room—and we would stand around the bed mostly, watching him or her breathe. They are usually in a hospital bed by then, not their own bed or a recliner, but a hospital bed because it has buttons and can go up and down," Fran explained. "At the end, the sheets on the bed are always stale. One time, there was blood on the top sheet, and no one had changed that top sheet. It is not hard to change a top sheet. The blood on that sheet bothered me."

"It would bother me," Mildred said.

"That time the daddy was close to dying. His name was Joe, but he was everybody's daddy." Fran caught her breath before she continued, remembering. "The breath gets kind of ragged, and they struggle, hanging on. And that is when we are supposed to tell someone in the family to assure the person struggling to breathe that it is all right to go on, but no one could listen to me. When I tried to tell them the words their daddy needed to hear, they couldn't listen. The family went to the kitchen to talk—they said to eat—but they were talking in the kitchen, so I leaned in and whispered the words Joe needed to hear."

Fran fell silent, remembering. Mildred waited.

"Do you know what I said?"

"You told him you loved him," Mildred said.

"That is right. I told Joe I loved him, and I wasn't lying or pretending even. I did love him. I only knew him a couple of weeks, and we never had a conversation that was what you and I think of as conscious, but we had been together."

"You loved Joe, and then you told him it was all right to go on."

"He was holding onto my hand and wouldn't let go though his eyes were closed, and he couldn't talk. I got so tired of standing I had to reach out with one foot and drag a chair over. But I didn't want to let go of his hand. That would have been too much. So, I dragged a chair over with my foot and finally sat down and breathed with him for a while," she said. "I wanted to change that soiled top sheet, but I could not let go of his hand because I loved him. After you say those words, you mean them in a way that you can't know when you only feel them as a habit or feel kindly toward someone. Did you know that saying the words *I love you* is powerful? So powerful. Anyway, I held his hand until the family came back. And his daughter looked daggers at me like she thought I was competing for his attention, but her daddy was already gone. Not dead. Gone. He lingered in the room in a way that you and I don't have a way to explain, and I got up and moved away from the bed and let the family gather. I saw the blood on the top sheet again, and I wanted to change it because there was still time. There were just three of them; and when he breathed his last, his daughter got very busy moving things around in the bedroom. And when the two men in the long black car came to transport her father, she got upset because his hair wasn't combed. She looked hard at me, as if it was my fault, and so I found a comb in the bathroom drawer and combed Joe's hair for his daughter. She needed her daddy's hair combed, but she couldn't do it."

"You could do it," Mildred said, not surprised.

"She was trying not to cry, too, so she was snuffling. Muffling the screams that wanted to come out. You know that sound?"

"Yes. I know that sound." Mildred felt that she was about to start making that sound herself.

"Mama. Daddy. Sister. Husband. My love. My only love. My sweetheart. My darling. I have heard all the good-byes people can make."

"I imagine you have." Mildred had heard a few herself, because you don't have to be a volunteer at hospice to spend time by dying people in beds at home and the hospital.

"And I have seen the people who have been caregivers for so long that they don't have a gasp of air left in them to say good-bye. Before anyone comes to get the person who has passed, we pull a sheet up over them. You can't do that too quickly. You have to wait until the time is right to pull the sheet up. But after that, you wait for the people to come with the big black car. And while you are waiting you begin to imagine that the sheet might move or the wind could catch it and lift it up and that you were wrong. You don't completely believe that underneath that sheet there is no more motion. No heartbeat. No breath. Nothing. I wonder if it will be like that for Belle sometime."

"Sam is going through a hard time, but he doesn't seem to be getting any worse."

"He will one day," Fran said, facing the truth. "I thought I would be here to help Belle through that." Fran shook her head to erase the false image she had held of herself and a different future with Sam and Belle.

"I always thought I would outlive everybody. I honestly thought that."

Mildred did not think about her own death often. Whatever pain occurred for others from her eventual permanent absence, it would not last long.

"Winston will be all right," Fran predicted. "He has lived long enough without me not to be devastated at my passing, but it might be hard for him if it happens in the next few weeks or months. You will look after Winston for me, won't you?"

Mildred wanted to ask: *What if I'm not here? What if I just disappear?* That could happen, too.

For Mildred Budge had often thought that one could simply evaporate into thin air all of a sudden without leaving a trace of what had occurred, and that idea had appealed to her more than once. She was here, and then she was gone. A vapor! And that is what happens to vapors.

"I will look out for Winston. He will not starve. He will not be lonely. He can sit beside us at church."

"Us," Fran repeated the word dolefully. "It is a wonderful word, isn't it? Us? It is what everyone wants. To belong as part of an us. You and I have been an us. Winston and I are an us. The church...."

"The church is the place for people who are finding ways to belong and do belong in all kinds of vaporish ways," Mildred murmured. And then a part of her that she had shushed a long, long time ago began to keen inside of her: *Please don't go. Wait until after I have disappeared. If you have to leave, go then.*

But Mildred Budge did not let those words become breath. They stopped at her heart and froze, stored inside with all of the other sounds that you keep locked inside of you. Screams, occasionally. But there had been songs of praise that welled up in her, too, and which she had sealed inside herself—not because she couldn't sing love songs to God but because some words were so very intimate and private that one kept them inside, precious and protected.

"I am being morbid. I am just going in for a biopsy. It may be nothing. But, Millie, even if it is nothing this time, there will be another day, another problem to solve. You have to face the truth. You know what you and I have always said about trouble."

"It is not what you are looking for that kills you. Something else happens. How long will it take to get the results of the biopsy?"

"A day or two. A week. You know they don't like to tell you a definite time exactly, and they will call me. I'm not to call them for at least a week."

"They don't get in a hurry."

"Well, it's not an emergency, and the hospital personnel are overworked. Everybody everywhere is tired these days."

Mildred, who had begun her day in joy and started it by praying for joy to overtake everyone because it was real, could hardly move her neck in that moment, the muscles were so tight. No Tylenol or even a long walk would ease that tension.

"Winston's going to take me over to the hospital first thing in the morning. I think it is going to hurt," Fran predicted.

"It will, but the pain won't last long," Mildred confirmed because it is best to acknowledge pain, for when you do the accompanying fear diminishes, and the pain is lessened somehow.

"Do you know what I miss right now in this moment?" Fran asked suddenly.

"Gritz?" Mildred asked, between breaths. The question just popped out of her mouth. Mildred knew that her best friend had loved her first husband long and truly, and maybe Fran wanted to say his name out loud to someone in the solitary moment called talking about cancer and a biopsy. You couldn't easily do that with your second husband, still a newlywed and not fully aware of all the words and feelings that have shaped you into the lover you are today.

It was Gritz's death that had caused Fran to become a volunteer with hospice. And then after Fran had started dating Winston, she had given up her volunteer duties to have more time to be in love with Winston.

Fran was not shaken by Mildred's question. Gritz was part of who she was—not really the past at all. He always would be. Everyone you ever loved was always part of your present.

"It is odd how you miss people you have adored. Just adored. I loved Gritz, and a part of me that Winston doesn't even know still does. But I am not being unfaithful to either one of them. Sometimes, when Winston holds my hand I can feel Gritz in the clasp, and it is not wrong. Though it is an odd thing to say out loud. I know that," Fran said. "But we all know a lot of things that we don't say out loud and which are true as can be."

"Love goes on," Mildred agreed, though she wasn't sure of what she was saying. It had been a while since someone had held her hand.

"What I miss most right now is our business. I miss being able to plan our business. I want to work. I am not through working. But maybe I was wrong to take Liz's booth. Maybe I was wrong," Fran said with wonder and a tinge of something that sounded like regret. "I have such high hopes for it. For us. We are not through being us— businesswomen with a future."

"You can still have high hopes," Mildred replied automatically.

Fran was talking more to herself than to Mildred or even Gritz, for she talked to her first husband often when alone, but the two old friends often eavesdropped on one another's innermost thoughts—prayers, too-- and called that a conversation.

"I have a pretty clear idea about breast cancer and how long you can expect to live and all kinds of other things when they hang a diagnosis on you. But you know and I know...."

Fran almost didn't finish making plain what both women knew; and in that moment, Mildred Budge could not read

Fran's thoughts. She did not know what Fran needed her to know in that moment. In her absolute helplessness to rescue her friend, Mildred Budge swallowed hard the knowledge of her own inadequacy to do anything really other than keep her company while she talked and hurt and missed her first husband, was concerned about her new husband, and still wanted to be a go-getter businesswoman.

"Do you know what hospice patients say they want out of life when the end is coming?"

Mildred did know the answer because Fran had told her many times through the years, referencing different people, different couples, mamas and daddies and their children. The situation changed. The people changed. But the same desire was present in all of them. She had heard it many times, but Fran needed to say the words again to relive the truth, so Mildred nodded for her to *go ahead, tell me.*

"They want a bowl of ice cream after supper and to watch their favorite television show. On the weekends, they want to watch a football game. That is what people want when they are dying. And we can have that all the time if we remember. All the time. Every day, we can have something as simple as a bowl of ice cream or watch *Everybody Loves Raymond* or a game--some game."

Fran liked to watch *Jeopardy* at 4:30 in the afternoon, but she didn't say that now because she and Gritz had watched it together, and she had not yet figured out if watching *Jeopardy* with Winston was right or wrong. The idea was so tender inside of her that Fran could not even say the words to herself, let alone to her best friend.

"Is that third booth too much for you? Until I can, well, help? Is it too much, Mildred?"

"We will figure it out as we go," Mildred promised.

"Winston may be preoccupied."

"I can solve any problem that arises," Mildred said confidently.

"Do you know what I want when I get home?" Fran said.

"A bowl of ice cream?" Mildred guessed.

"No. I want the trash bags we have been using at Winston's house to be gone. Winston bought the kind that has a scent, and I can't stand the smell. If I need chemo, I am really going to hate that smell."

"We can take care of that," Mildred promised delicately. She was not yet comfortable in Winston's home. The three times she had been there, she had felt like a guest. She preferred to visit the couple when they were sleeping at Fran's house.

"I don't want Winston to think...."

"That you are hard to live with. Hard to please."

"That I am high maintenance."

"I know."

And there it was, though people said that differently. *I don't want to be a burden. I don't want you to give up your life to take care of me. I don't want scented trash bags.*

As if she hadn't heard her, Fran continued, "I don't ever want to eat any other kind of cheese than Sargento. I bought Sargento cheese on sale one day, and it was so much better than the brand we grew up with that I didn't even know cheese could taste that good."

"Sargento cheese is good," Mildred agreed. She had other kinds of cheese in her fridge. She bought whatever was on sale: buy one, get one.

"I know you buy what is on sale and I have, too. But my Winston likes his morning eggs scrambled with cheese, and I want Winston to have the best cheese, and the best cheese is Sargento. I am going to stop on my way home and buy a pound of Sargento cheese," Fran declared, and in the declaration, she was prophesying, 'I'll be here for a future with Winston of scrambled eggs with cheese.'

"He will like that," Mildred promised though it had been her experience that most men didn't care one way or the other about good or better cheese. They just want to eat.

"He probably won't notice the difference. But if he could tell the difference, he would know that I got him the best kind. The very best kind of cheese. From now on, Winston only eats Sargento cheese," Fran pledged. It was a new vow on top of her recent wedding vows and just as important in its way. It was a heart's promise and a prophecy all in one.

"Do you know how much you love Sister Schubert cinnamon rolls?" Fran asked suddenly, her thoughts darting.

"I have two packages in my freezer right now," Mildred said. Sister Schubert rolls in your freezer was like money in the bank.

"Soon, I am going to take you over to that bakery in the shopping center and buy you a vanilla cinnamon roll. They are better than Sister Schubert's cinnamon rolls. I have known that for a while, and I haven't gotten around to telling you. I'm sorry about that. You deserve better than that from me."

"Let's go right now to that bakery. Let's buy all the cinnamon rolls in the case and eat them for lunch and freeze the rest for later," Mildred proposed recklessly.

It was a way of staying away from home longer.

Fran's voice grew somber and tired. "Your fellows are inside, and Winston is waiting at home. The biopsy tomorrow is going to hurt, isn't it?" Fran asked again.

"Yes," Mildred said. "But you can manage pain, and you won't be doing it alone."

"We both want to run away from home," Fran concluded, finally pushing open her door. She shifted her body in order to lower herself out and down. Moving toward The Emporium, she had bounded down. Headed home with a stop at the new rental house on the way, Fran moved more slowly, managing her sighs as she went.

"I am going to check the mailbox," Mildred said.

Fran waited at the front door as Mildred opened the mailbox and retrieved all the flyers and sales pitches for hearing aids, car insurance, and credit cards that still showed up at this address even though the occupants had been gone for almost a half year.

"Just trash," Mildred explained.

"This is such a great house," Fran approved when Mildred joined her at the front door. "If you make up your mind to be happy about it, you and your crew could be comfortable living here."

"It is a practical solution to my problem of overcrowding in the bungalow, only I just can't see myself living here."

"Oh, Millie. You sleep at your other house, but you already live here."

9

TEACHABLE MOMENTS

In the garage, two pairs of legs were jutting out from under the front of the old green Mercedes that had come with the house.

Mildred had considered asking the real estate agent to get the old car hauled off as part of the closing costs of the sale, but Jake had stopped her. He was retiring from the university as the man in charge of facilities, and needing a project that would help him adjust to his new freedom, he and Chase were bringing the old car back to life.

"Let the boy and me work on it. I can show him a few things," he suggested, and Chase had liked the car and the packed garage. Chase liked working with his hands. He didn't mind getting dirty either.

A light moved underneath the big green car.

"Give us a minute, Millie. Chase and I are checking for leaks."

"They are checking for leaks," Fran repeated to Mildred, as if she hadn't heard.

"We are looking for markers like stains and damp spots. Oil. Radiator. Antifreeze. Hang tight."

The beam from the flashlight roamed around under the car while two pairs of legs jiggled this way and that.

"Hang tight," Mildred repeated this time to Fran.

"I am hanging tight," she said. "But I am going to go wash my hands."

Mildred nodded, wondering if she needed to stay in the garage with the boys or retreat and leave them to their leak checking.

"No leaks," Jake concluded, as he said something to Chase, who immediately began to wiggle out on his back from under the car.

Jake followed suit, sliding along on a piece of stretched brown cardboard that had once been an Amazon Prime delivery box, which he had broken down to be an insulating glider and protector for them from the dirty garage floor. They stood up at the same time with Jake brushing off the back of Chase and then himself.

Chase spoke up. "I checked the oil with the dip stick. Dip stick. Dip stick."

"We are about to learn how to use this wrench," Jake boasted, holding up the tool he needed to loosen the oil cap underneath.

"The oil falls out slow," Chase said, his eyes wide and his speech slowed as if matching it to the dripping pace of the draining oil. But he was talking. Her boy was talking in whole sentences. And there was a light in his eyes.

Mildred closed her own, swaying with the knowledge that Chase was coming up from the deep without her inevitably, as if his getting better and becoming whole could not be stopped. She rested in that realization.

Jake was helping Chase do that, and she had never been more grateful in her life to anyone.

"You don't care if we use that old dish pan over there, do you, Mildred? It won't be good for anything else after that.

Dirty oil makes a terrible mess," Jake explained. "You almost can't clean it up. You just have to throw out what you used. You will lose the dish pan if we use it."

Jake wiped his hands on a cloth from his back pocket. He handed the cloth to Chase who copied his motions. Overhead, a lone light bulb swung from a long dangling cord.

"Use anything you like," she urged.

"It is a great car, Mildred," Jake said with satisfaction. He brushed his open palms on the sides of his khaki coveralls, an old-fashioned thick-cloth garment that you stepped into and zipped up.

It is a great car," Chase repeated.

"The boyo and I will have it going in no time," Jake promised. "We will go for a spin all together." He grinned, imagining the future.

"Hi, Fran," he said when she returned, drying her hands on a paper towel.

He pointed to the trash can, and she used it.

"Fran, you are coming with us in the car when it is ready. Winston, too. We will do the town together. I am almost officially retired. There will be time now for drives in the country in classic cars with your friends. This boy is a natural with cars," Jake repeated proudly.

Chase had the flashlight they had been using to inspect the underside of the car, and he was aiming the beam here and there in the garage, finding tools hanging on walls and spider webs in the corners.

"A natural," she repeated, as Chase looked up at her, and switched off the light. The hand-me-down flannel shirt he had put on that morning had a couple of greasy dark stains, and there was a tear in his pants.

They were the happiest two people Mildred had seen in a long time, and the experience of morning's joy returned.

Fran was having a biopsy tomorrow. And Mildred was standing in a burgeoning joy once again, rising up in her like a refreshing spring of water.

"What are you looking at us like that for?" Jake asked, cocking his head quizzically. His eyes were smiling.

Mildred Budge couldn't answer him, for in that moment something happened to her that had only recently happened to Fran at The Emporium. She really saw Jake, and just like Fran had with Streeter an hour ago, she fell a little in love with him.

He grinned at her. "Are you girls hungry?" he asked. "Because we are," he said, his eyes registering the change in Mildred but not understanding it.

Transfixed, Mildred could not speak--not a word.

Fran reached out and touched her elbow. Mildred registered the touch, and she knew what it meant. *Let's not ruin this moment with talk of lumps and biopsies.*

"How do you feel about fried bologna?" Jake asked.

"I forget about bologna, but a fried bologna sandwich sounds good. Mighty good," Fran said, clapping her hands together with appetite. "Show me where there is a frying pan."

"No, ma'am. You are back from your honeymoon where they were waiting on you hand and foot, and that is what is going to happen to you here with Chase and me. You girls come with us," he invited, as Mildred Budge watched and listened, absorbed by the sight and sound of him and the boy he was teaching to work with his hands.

Jake smiled warmly, shaking his head, confused but not minding that Mildred could not take her eyes off him.

"Chase and I will show you how it's done," Jake said, leading the way to the kitchen. You girls come into the kitchen and sit over there on those bar stools and watch. Chase, wash your hands with soap, and then get the ladies a cold drink from the fridge. Chase and I bring our own root beer because we like it better than Gatorade."

Her boy didn't wash his hands first, but Chase did go to the old fridge and extract two cold root beers. "Get one for yourself, and then wash those hands with soap, buddy," Jake said, searching in the kitchen cabinet for a skillet. Jake didn't mind repeating himself to Chase. He understood about how people hear and how long it takes for some people to find the meaning in words aimed in their direction.

Jake opened and closed two cabinets before he found an old skillet. He rinsed it off, drying it swiftly with a paper napkin from a stack on the table Mildred had left when she had first bought the house and found herself stealing thirty minutes for herself looking at the world through a different window and eating a package of peanut butter crackers instead of a ham sandwich at home.

"How many?" Jake asked, as he adjusted the heat on the electric stove.

"How many what?" Mildred asked, wanting to wash her hands but comfortable where she was and not wanting to leave the room. Some kind of spell had come upon her, and she didn't want to break it.

"Slices of bologna do you want?" Jake asked, casting a quick glance in her direction. His gaze grew quizzical.

"However many slices you are having," she replied, though the exact answer would be three. Mildred always ate three pieces of bologna on two fold-overs, splitting the third piece to make the sandwich meatier.

Jake grinned. "It will take ten minutes tops. Come over here, Chase, and learn how a man cooks. First thing we do is peel off this red string here." He showed him how. "Once the skillet gets hot the bologna will start to curl up, and we don't want it to do that because we want the whole slice of bologna to cook, edges too. So, we are going to make cuts like this at the edge."

Using a butter knife from the kitchen drawer, Jake demonstrated how to nick the edges of the bologna so that it would lie flat in the skillet while searing. "See how it makes little wings all the way around? That is all you need to know about frying bologna, except keep an eye on it. Even if it burns, it's still pretty good."

"I like it burned," Fran piped up. She was watching them carefully, taking quick breaths of air. Perched beside Mildred on another kitchen stool, she was in no mood to leave now.

Jake nodded in her direction. "Great minds...."

Soon the mouthwatering aroma of searing thick slices of bologna filled the kitchen, as enticing in its way as the aroma of charcoal briquettes when someone is outside at twilight grilling hot dogs.

Mildred's mouth watered, and the tension in her shoulders began to ease. Her root beer was icy cold. "I haven't had one of these in ages," she confessed, her body growing easeful. The vinyl-cushioned bar stool was pretty comfortable. Her feet reached the bottom foot rest, and the back of the stool held her steady. She sat taller on the kitchen stool than she did in the chairs at her own home, and she liked the view.

Jake fried the whole package of bologna in under ten minutes and settled the loaded paper plate with the steaming slices down on the island in front of her. He opened the loaf of bread, twisting the plastic tie with nimble fingers. "We are not standing on ceremony. God is good," he said, his informal blessing said with a smile. Then, tipping his own cold root beer toward them, he toasted, "Here's to us. Help yourself," he invited, stepping back to let Chase go first.

Eye level with the counter top and the fixings, Chase used a paper napkin to place his bread on and then using both hands squeezed too much mustard on the bread.

"Live and learn," Jake said, flashing a grin.

They made fried bologna fold-overs using only mustard, which dripped and made a mess. They laughed at the mess.

"Chase and I haven't finished with the car. Otherwise, we would be driving you home in it," Jake said. "When he gets taller and his feet can touch the pedals...." Jake began, his idea fading away, and for a fleeting moment, he was embarrassed to be heard planning a future that no one had heard before. His eyes darted self-consciously to Mildred.

"That old car won't be here when Chase is old enough to learn to drive," Mildred said.

"I don't know why you think that," Jake countered immediately. "These old classics will last as long as you want to take care of them. We are going to take it for a test drive soon. Chase and I. You girls coming with us?" he asked, repeating his invitation.

Mildred nodded, yes, taking a bite of her sandwich and holding it with her napkin. The sandwich was hot and tasty, and she was hungry.

"You want me to run you home in the Expedition before we get back at it," Jake offered, balling up his used paper napkin. Chase imitated him.

"It is not far," Mildred said. "I need a walk anyway."

"I will take you," Fran offered. "I'm not in a hurry to get home."

"I thought you needed to go to the store and buy some cheese."

"I am still here," she replied inscrutably. "I will take Millie home," Fran told Jake, finishing her fold-over. She patted her lips and turned her attention to the drink. "Winston would have liked that," Fran said. She looked around as if he might suddenly appear at the back door looking for her.

"The boy and I will finish up in the garage and be along then. We have to clean up after ourselves. What time do you want me to pick you up later, Millie?"

Mildred didn't know what Jake was talking about.

"For my retirement party. You and the boy are coming. You haven't forgotten?" he asked quickly, eyeing her with a sudden suspicion.

"We will be about an hour," Jake said. "The party starts at three, but we ought to get there fifteen minutes early, don't you think? I figure somebody will be nervous about me showing up. And I am the guest of honor."

As he talked, Jake watched Mildred's face. It was coming back to her—this party. She knew she had been forgetting something. Her eyes widened as she realized what it was.

He spoke more slowly. "Mildred, I want you to meet my friends. Columbia Wren, in particular."

"Columbia Wren," Mildred repeated, standing up. Just that quickly, the bologna was not agreeing with her. The carbonation in the root beer was creating a pressure in the middle of her chest. Or maybe she was about to have a heart attack.

Fran spoke up. "Millie, I want to show you something in the master bedroom before we go. Boys, you get on back to work. And thanks for lunch, Jake. We will be heading out in a little while, but Millie and I need to take care of some business in the back of the house first."

Jake did not argue with Fran. His hand on the back of Chase's neck, Jake steered the boy toward the garage and the wrench they were going to learn how to use next.

1 0

PARTY TIME

"You forgot the party," Fran said, after she and Mildred had retreated to the master bedroom.

Mildred had not spent much time in this bedroom. Though she had bought the house lock, stock and barrel, standing in the master bedroom felt like an invasion of the previous owner's privacy.

Fran did not feel the same way.

"We need to move fast. Don't fight me on this," Fran warned.

Mildred couldn't say anything. *Was she losing her mind?* Sam's condition could have begun this way.

"How could you have forgotten Jake's retirement party?" Fran wondered, more to herself than to Mildred. And before her friend could offer a limp explanation, Fran declared, "You are going to that party, and you are not going to use worrying about me or feeling tired as an excuse to get out of it."

Mildred was trying to figure out how to get out of it.

"Jake has been there for you," Fran reminded her. "Over and over again. He asked you to go to his retirement party. He expects you to be there for him in front of his friends. And he wants the boy there, too. Jake will get Chase home in time to clean up, and that will take ten minutes, tops. It is going to take you longer."

"I am a mess, and I did forget the party," Mildred admitted. "Jake's retirement party. Do you think he could tell that I had forgotten?"

Fran considered the question. "Yep," she said finally. "He saw it on your face about the same time I did. That is why he took Chase back to the garage to give you time to figure out what you are going to wear. He has that much sense, and don't worry. Jake doesn't hold a grudge. That's rare in anybody."

"I knew I was forgetting something, but I couldn't think of what it was."

Mildred did not add that she had remembered that she was forgetting something. All morning, something had been nagging at her, but she could not put her finger on what it was.

Fran waved away Mildred's explanation.

"At least you were invited. Jake didn't invite us to his retirement party," Fran said, her voice slightly aggrieved at what she was actively choosing to consider an oversight.

Having just praised Jake's lack of grudge-holding, Fran's position of being offended seemed paradoxical.

"Only because Jake thought you were going to be on your honeymoon," Mildred reminded her immediately, though she had not discussed the invitation list of the party or who else would be there.

Other than being kicked out of the Lunch Bunch for getting married, Fran was always invited to every party.

"If Jake had invited us, we could have said *no*. But he assumed a *no* just because we were out of town. I guess he was just being logical. I invited him to my wedding though."

Mildred stared disbelievingly at Fran. Jake's invitation to the wedding was not personal. The whole church had been invited to Fran's wedding. "I am sure you can go if you want to," Mildred said.

She had no right to invite Fran, but the wounded quality in Fran's eyes caused Mildred to speak before she could think it through.

"No. I can't go to a party today, and you know why. I just got back from my honeymoon, and I have got stuff to do. I don't have time to go to the party."

Mildred grew wordless. Two hours and a half wasn't much time.

"You are going to that party, and you are going for both of us. I love a party," Fran sniffed. "It is an afternoon thing so you don't need a cocktail dress."

"I have never in my life owned a cocktail dress," Mildred said. And the dress she had bought for Fran's wedding was too--too something. It had too much cloth. The golden dress was right for a wedding, but it was wrong for a retirement party among strangers at a university where, she assumed, everyone was more sophisticated than she had ever been in her life. Smarter, too. Better educated. Better at making small talk.

"Did Jake even tell me about his retirement party?" Fran asked suddenly. "I don't even think I knew about it. Was he keeping it a secret? I would have reminded you about the party if I had known about it."

Fran faced Mildred, who sat down heavily on the foot of the queen-size bed. The bed covering was an old-fashioned quilted blanket with a design of purple and yellow flowers and plush with natural cotton batting that is soft and cozy. She liked it. There was something written on the far bottom corner of the blanket. Mildred leaned over and squinted. It was the quilter's name: Julie Helms.

"No one was keeping any secrets," Mildred assured her. She was growing more and more still, not from panic but from the kind of inertia that comes upon you when you realize that you must do something you don't want to do, and there is no escape. That was most often true of funeral-going, but a retirement party fit into that category, too.

"I know your clothes, and nothing you have in your closet at home is right for a retirement party," Fran said, studying Mildred's face while she thought about what her friend had hanging in her closet. "Not your grocery-store clothes, your Walmart-shopping clothes, your going-to-the-doctor clothes, your Sunday-morning clothes or your Sunday-Vespers clothes. If you still went to wedding showers, something like that might do," Fran mused, shaking her head.

"But I don't go to wedding showers anymore not because I wouldn't, but because women our age may get married, but they don't have showers anymore and even their daughters are already married. I haven't bought a going-to-a wedding shower outfit in years. I meant to call that lady in Georgia where I bought my dress for your wedding and order a going-to-a-retirement-party-at-a-university outfit, but I forgot. That lady would have known what to send. She knew clothes and occasions, and she assured me that she could ship me an outfit for any occasion in forty-eight hours. I just never got around to calling her."

Mildred couldn't remember where she had placed that woman's business card with the phone number on it, and she couldn't think of her name either. *How could she have misplaced such a valuable piece of information?*

She knew right where the numbers were for the trash collectors when she could not remember which holidays they were observing and when to put her trash can out on the street, and she had that hard-to-find phone number for the waterworks inspector. Sometimes, when she ran the tap water at eight o'clock at night to fill the coffeepot well for the next morning, the tap water smelled funny. Sometimes—not every time—she called the water inspector the next day about that suspicious smell, and he always told her the same thing: 'Let the water run a little while when that happens. It is just some chemicals we use to clean it up. The smell will dissipate. The water is safe to drink.'

That advice never set well with Mildred Budge. Never. Just remembering the inspector's words caused her to feel peeved in the same way that Fran was feeling peeved, too.

"After you came home with that dress from that shop in Georgia, I thought you and I would make a daytrip and go shopping there sometime. Just because I got married doesn't mean we can't go shopping or take a trip whenever we want to." Fran stared off into space as if she were looking at her calendar and considering which day the two of them could take a daytrip to Georgia.

"We can go sometime," Mildred agreed. But she didn't know when they could fit it into their respective schedules.

Liz Luckie had driven her car that day of shopping for a dress for Fran's wedding, and Mildred had been staring out the window. She did not remember the route to that shop exactly. You head toward Atlanta, and take a right on a road before you got there. About twenty miles later you take another road off the beaten path. Mildred could clearly recall how to get from the clothing store to that restaurant where they had fried chicken livers and an old-fashioned pastry case by the checkout register that contained whole cakes, pies, and cream horns. That was very clear in her mind. But she did not remember how to get to the dress store itself on that small hill that was atop that long winding road that led up to the big old house that was a store simply called *A Dress For You*.

Mildred began to worry about finding out the directions to that dress shop in Georgia without having to ask Liz Luckie, who would want to go, too, when Fran snapped her fingers in front of Mildred.

"Not now. Don't go there in your head now. You have got a bigger problem, and it is much more pressing. You need something to wear to Jake's party, and I know how we can get you dressed lickety-split."

Lickety-split did not sound promising to Mildred Budge.

Lickety-split sounded like being in too much of a hurry, and she hated to rush.

"My hair...." Mildred said, suddenly, reaching around to touch the back of her limp curls. It was too long. She was a couple of weeks overdue for a haircut. She had been postponing calling the hairdresser, too.

"We are going to have to work with what we have. You need to look your best for Jake's sake."

"Will anybody be looking at me really?" Mildred asked hopefully. "Won't they be talking to Jake? I will just be standing around holding a cup of punch. I wonder what kind of punch it will be. Probably not lime sherbet with ginger ale. It will probably be something with sparkling grape juice. People at a university will want something more sophisticated than ginger ale. They will probably serve that sparkling grape juice. That is what it will probably be."

Fran snapped her fingers in front of Mildred's face again. "Not now. Come back to the moment! This is not about the punch. We have got to get you dressed fast. Then, we have to get the boy home and cleaned up."

"Chase has got a pair of Sunday slacks and a shirt with a collar. He just needs a bath."

"You told me yourself that the boy knows how to take a shower. Jake will get him home in time. Don't worry about the boy. Let's concentrate on you. Chase we can handle. And you are wrong. People will be looking you over. And do you know why?"

"Because I don't work there, and they won't recognize me?" Mildred asked. She was tempted to fall back on the bed where she was sitting and close her eyes. You can blank out the world with your eyes closed if you know how.

"No. It is because you will be with Jake, and they will all try to learn your name and look you over—not out of meanness. People just look each other over when they meet them for the first time. And, you are a white woman."

"What has that got to do with it?"

"Jake is not a white man."

"I forget what color we both are," Mildred said, brow wrinkling. Yes, she did forget skin colors. But there is so much the world expects you to remember, you have to let go of some things, don't you?

"Can you just trust me for a minute?" Fran asked, her gaze far off. She was thinking.

"I think I might need to tell Jake I can't go. Because look at me. I can't go looking like this. Jake deserves better than how I look."

"He doesn't deserve better than you. He does merit some preparation on your part."

"I meant to prepare," Mildred defended herself weakly.

"But you were thinking about Janie, the baby coming, Chase, Belle, and Sam who pops in a lot and this new house. Don't give in to panic right now. We can do this," Fran said.

She gripped Mildred by both shoulders. "Can you trust me?" she asked.

Mildred swallowed hard and wished she had a Rolaid. Maybe, two.

"Right over there is the closet of the woman who used to live here."

"A dead woman," Mildred said, looking at the closed closet door.

"Let's not hold that against her," Fran said.

11

AFTERNOON SOCIAL

"We are going to see what our sister in heaven has in here that will work today for this afternoon social. That is what we can call it. An afternoon social. And that is very simple to understand. All it means is that anything you wear is fine as long as you are not showing any cleavage. No cleavage!"

"I have never shown my cleavage ever, night or day."

Fran raised a single hand: *stop.* "I asked you to trust me."

Mildred Budge had no other choice but to trust Fran.

"Do what needs to be done," Mildred agreed sullenly. She let her weight settle on the foot of the bed, placing a hand on either side of her to test the resilience of the mattress. It was a good mattress. It wasn't a fancy mattress that sensed your body temperature and made itself hot or cold. And it wasn't one of those heavy foam mattresses that you could place an egg on and the egg would stay put.

"It is just an ordinary mattress," she said out loud to God, looking up at the ceiling. Saying the words comforted her. If the dead woman owned an ordinary mattress, what kind of clothes had she worn? Mildred closed her eyes, listening to Fran shoving metal hangers around in the dead woman's closet and talking to herself.

Surely a woman who slept on an ordinary mattress would have an ordinary outfit in her closet—one that she could borrow to wear to Jake's party. Please God.

Fran was shifting hangers in the closet, talking to herself but loudly enough for Mildred to hear her. "No. No. No. Maybe. Maybe. Maybe. Possibly. Possibly. Oh! Oh! And it is a three. A three would work."

Fran called out jubilantly, "She has got a nice assortment of threes!"

"That is good," Mildred approved, but she did not know how a three could be good news for her. She was bigger than any three she had ever thought about.

Fran returned with both hands holding hangers. "All of her pants have elastic in the waist. Don't we love this woman?"

"We do," Mildred agreed, weakly. She tried to look at the pants that Fran was holding up for display on their hangers.

"She has these taupe pants in a three. Won't that be a nice change?" Fran asked brightly. She waved the pants like a victory flag. They billowed slightly.

"Taupe pants in a three," Mildred repeated. The words meant nothing to her. "I wear a sixteen. A nice change from what?"

"A change from wearing black pants. The traditional outfit of ladies everywhere. Black pants and a top."

"Taupe pants and a top?" Mildred asked, but she was defeated and only repeating words. She felt hopeless, the words *taupe* and *three* were meaningless.

"That is what I am thinking," Fran said. Fran walked around Mildred and laid out the selected pieces of clothing on the bed behind her.

"Now, don't think *no* at first, because sometimes the word *no* is the first word that comes to your mind. Instead, think, *maybe,* and take a slow, optimistic look."

"I am looking," Mildred said, her eyes going from one piece of clothing to another.

"See anything you like?" Fran asked. She concentrated on the options, mentally assembling outfits for her friend in her mind.

Just as Mildred was about to point out a pair of shiny aqua pants, Fran grabbed them up. "You don't want to wear these. It is dark in that closet, and I didn't see the rhinestones running down the seam of each leg in the closet."

Fran hurriedly folded up the shiny pants, muttering under her breath, "Somebody got ahold of a Bedazzler."

Mildred watched with regret as Fran took away her possible future with the shiny pants. The rhinestones were what Mildred liked. She loved rhinestones.

"Check out these taupe pants," Fran suggested. "This is a good brand. They are Travelers."

Mildred squinted, questioningly.

"It is how Chico's markets their clothes. These pants are from Chico's, and the Travelers brand is for people who go places—upscale places like a university! -- and want to pack clothes that will not wrinkle."

Realizing what she had just said, Fran nodded up and down, reassuringly. "Mildred, these pants won't wrinkle. You can wear them all day long and all night too. You could sleep in them." She shrugged slightly. "It is a good brand."

How did Fran know so much about Travelers from a store she had not mentioned before?

In that moment, Mildred could not name the clothing store that Fran preferred; and when she thought about it, she knew the reason why. Except for her recent shopping mission to find a wedding dress, Fran was still wearing the same clothes she had always worn: classics from Talbots. Fran's clothes were high quality garments, and they lasted for years. That mattered. Fran hadn't gained a pound in twenty years.

Mildred's size had been going up for as long as she had been growing older. She used to wear an eight, and then she wore a ten. Now she was a fourteen on a slim day and a sixteen when she had eaten potato salad and a bowl of ice cream the night before. Just thinking about a bowl of ice cream made her want some.

"You want to wear those taupe pants," Fran decided. "They will fit you."

"How do you know that?"

"How do I know anything?" Fran asked, waiting for Mildred to answer that question.

Instead, Mildred asked her best friend, "Which top do I want to wear?"

There were three selected possible tops from the closet on the quilt cover, all of them in a brighter color than Mildred usually wore.

There was a white top with big red flowers on it. No. Mildred loved a red lipstick, but she didn't exactly like to wear red. She couldn't wear that bright montage of geometric shapes in front of other people. There was another blouse with oversized black and white squares interspersed with polka dots in various configurations.

"Do you think the woman liked to play dominos?" Mildred asked.

"I can see why you would think that," Fran said, scooping up the domino shirt. "This won't do. In the light of day, it looks like the kind of shirt men wear on a bowling league. No. No. I couldn't see so well in the closet. If none of these suit us, there are some more clothes in there." Fran turned as if to go into the dark abyss of the dead woman's closet one more time.

"That last shirt there with the small ruffle that goes up the neckline. It is okay. What do you think of that shirt?" Fran asked.

It was inoffensive.

"Would that shade of lavender go with the taupe pants?" Mildred asked.

"Of course, it would. Taupe and lavender are in the same family."

Mildred slumped then. She did not understand discussions of colors and families. Fran didn't try to justify that point of view or explain it any better. Instead, Fran respectfully folded the taupe pants and the lavender top and stacked them on the bed beside Mildred, patting them before making her next statement.

"You don't have any taupe shoes."

Mildred shook her head.

"Black shoes will have to be all right then," Fran decided, but there was misgiving in her voice and disappointment in her eyes. "Sometimes you just have to go with what you have."

"Not if you cancel," Mildred replied. She eyed the bedroom door and was considering just leaving, walking out the front door and going home and locking her own front door and not answering the telephone. She would have to explain later; but maybe by then, she would be able to answer questions.

"You hate parties, don't you?" Fran asked, but it was really a statement.

"I don't exactly hate them," Mildred said, though she wondered why anyone would want to submit to the cacophony of a social gathering when you could simply read a book in the comfort of your own home where you don't have to make small talk.

"Which parts do you dislike the most? It helps to know what it is you really don't like."

"Finding a parking spot," Mildred said immediately. "On a big college campus where I don't know which building I am supposed to go into, I don't know where to park. Then, when I get inside, I immediately want to know where the ladies' room is; and once I find that, I hope there won't be a big mirror in there. If there is, I try to not look that way. I don't mind a mirror over the sink, where you can check your lipstick and teeth, but I just don't like a full-length mirror in a public restroom."

"No one does that I know of. People don't think that through when they install full-length mirrors in bathrooms. I have scared myself a few times. There are places where one does not want to see one's self so completely.

"We cannot control that. But you don't need to worry about parking. Jake's going to pick up you and Chase. He will know where to park. Jake probably has a designated parking space of his own. That will be nice. And a ladies' room will be near the party room because the party room will be a meeting room, and people who design buildings with rooms for meetings always put the restrooms nearby."

"I don't like signing a guest book when I first go in either."

"Signing a guest book happens at funerals. I don't think there will be one of those. And why do you not like that? It is just signing your name."

"I don't like to sign the roll in Sunday school either. I stopped signing that roll a while back."

"Oh, honey. Ever since you retired you don't like to give an accounting of where you are. It is like some kind of allergic reaction to people knowing your schedule. Sometimes you need to admit who and where you are. You can always write your name in very small scrunched up letters that are hard to read. And never put your address down. Just skip over that part. That is what I do."

Mildred didn't know why she hadn't thought of signing her name the way a doctor would. Yes. Yes, that would work. Though her vanity would be bruised when others saw her handwriting. She had excellent penmanship, and many people had praised her for it.

"Then there will be a big buffet table and you have to make a little plate of snacks and hold a cup of punch while your purse is swinging, and it could hit something. While you are doing that, you often have to talk to someone. I don't like to make small talk."

"I have noticed that about you," Fran said. "But it is not a failing. You just don't like to make small talk."

"Small talk is dangerous. It is so easy to get into trouble when you are talking without a purpose."

"If you find yourself talking to someone else, try to get the other person to do all the talking. Go on the offensive. Be nosy."

"See? That's one of the things I am afraid of appearing to be--nosy."

"Call it being friendly. Be friendly and curious. Dale Carnegie helped me with that problem a long time ago."

"You are good at small talk. It is one of the reasons we always sit together for church suppers and ladies' luncheons."

"I know. You like for me to do the small talking at tables." Fran hesitated.

Suddenly, they were discussing something more important. After the biopsy tomorrow, Fran would most likely not be going to social suppers and church luncheons. Mildred would have to make her own small talk for a while.

"You will do fine if I am not there. You have always let me do the talking, but you can talk. You used to work out in the world, and I am sure you did some small talking that you don't remember. It will come back to you. If someone asks you what you do now, tell them about your newest Sunday school lesson you are working on. I imagine people at a university would love to hear a lesson plan on any subject. Aren't you working on your next Sunday school lesson?"

Mildred nodded, dumbly. She had started the lesson for Teacher's Choice day just that morning, but the morning felt like a long time ago.

"I will be talking to professors who have written books and who know Jake in a way I don't really know Jake. I don't even know why he invited me. I don't belong there." Mildred began to lose heart.

"Oh, Mildred. You and Chase are Jake's family now. He invited his family to the retirement party. Now you go into that bathroom and splash some water on your face and slip into this new ensemble, and we will see if it works. I think it is going to be all right. That said, I am going to make another run through the closet for backups. But you go try that outfit on first."

Standing slowly, Mildred carried the taupe pants and lavender top with ruffles to the bathroom. Closing the lid of the toilet, she sat down and wriggled out of her Emporium work pants and slipped into the taupe britches. She liked the feel of the cloth. She stood up. The pants legs were a couple of inches too long. But she could stand and sit in them. She took off her Emporium work shirt and laid it on the counter and eyed the lavender top. She got one arm in it, and the sleeve was not too tight on her shoulder. She got the other arm in, and avoiding looking at herself in the mirror, Mildred fastened all of the buttons. Then she looked at herself in the mirror. The color suited her brown hair and dark eyes.

"I don't look horrible," she said, exhaling.

But her hair didn't look very good. She patted both sides of it to no avail. Her curls were limp. The swoop of bangs that usually framed her face was sweat-flattened against her forehead.

She came out for Fran to take in the effect, holding out both arms for Fran to see how the blouse fit. Mildred couldn't read her best friend's expression at first. Fran was concentrating. Then, purposefully, she walked over to

Mildred, reached under the shirt, and taking hold of the pants' waistband, she rolled them over at the waist, effectively shortening the pants so that the hem of each leg crested the top of Mildred's foot.

Stepping back, Fran approved of what she saw. "They are too long. You might trip on them. That will do until you can hem them."

"Maybe I could tape the hem up when I get home," Mildred suggested.

Fran ignored the idea.

"Like I said, that's a good brand. No wrinkles. Pretty colors. And it's free."

"Not exactly. I bought a whole house and what was inside came with it."

"Still," Fran said with a shrug. "You look nice. We need to do something about your hair. When is the last time you twisted it up?"

"I only tack up my hair when I am sweaty and plan to wash it later."

"You are sweaty, and I am sure you are planning to wash it later, but you don't have time right now to do that and curl it. Let me look in that woman's bathroom drawer."

Mildred stood stock still, listening while Fran opened and closed bathroom drawers, coming out at last with a tortoise shell comb, so old-fashioned Mildred had forgotten they had ever existed.

"Twist up your hair the way you do when you are mopping the floor."

Mildred reached behind her, grabbed a handful of hair and twisted it in a small knot.

"Hold it. Hold it. Hold it," Fran said as she reached up and pressed the tortoise shell comb down, holding the hair. She came around Mildred and using her fingers loosened a wisp of curling hair at one side and then the other.

"You should wear this style more often. It gives you cheekbones. I mean, really. You look thinner in the face this way," Fran said.

"Thinner?" Mildred asked, hope coming all of a sudden. *Thinner. Thinner. Thinner.*

She walked to the bathroom and surveyed the transformation. "I don't look horrible," she assured her reflection.

Appearing behind her, Fran grinned and met her gaze in the mirror. "You don't. You really don't look horrible. Now make up your mind to go to the party and have fun."

Mildred didn't say the word fun any more often than she used the word thinner about herself. Trying to smile at her reflection in the dead woman's mirror, Mildred practiced the idea, "I like fun. And I am going to go get some."

"You can do it," Fran encouraged. "I believe in you."

1 2

WONDER YEARS

The first white mouse that scurried past Mildred's feet did not seem like it could be real, but one suppressed squeal and a heartbeat later, another white mouse scampered across the beige carpeted floor in the Bishop-Parker room at the university, did a quick detour under the buffet table, and ran toward the black grand piano.

There was no one to elbow—to nudge and ask, "Did you see that mouse? Mice?"

But others saw. And, curiously, they just ignored what they saw.

Anchored in place by the peer pressure not to over-react, Mildred stood her ground, looking around for Chase, who had gone over to the grand piano partially covered in a red and gold fringed tapestry.

Mildred saw Chase fight the urge to stoop and crawl under the piano and go after the mouse. But he didn't.

Instead, he went over to Jake, who was talking politely to two colleagues, two women younger and better dressed than Mildred Budge. They were holding glass flutes, and when Mildred looked closer, it wasn't sparkling grape juice they were drinking. It was golden bubbling champagne.

Mildred began to wend her way toward Jake and Chase, pretending her feet might not run into a mouse, when she was stopped by an authoritative tap on her shoulder.

"Hello, I am Columbia Wren. And, you are Jake's friend. I am, too," she said smiling, as Mildred turned to greet her.

Dr. Wren was wearing a simple shift-like grey dress with an ivory cameo brooch on her left shoulder just above her name tag that introduced her. Dr. Wren was the vice president of the university.

"I am Mildred Budge," she affirmed forthrightly. *See, Fran? I can admit who I am, though I am not signing a ledger.*

"I know who you are. Jake talks about you. I envy your name. Budge. It is so optimistic. You are good at budging."

"From time to time," Mildred replied. "They aren't very big budges, but I am capable of change."

"I hear you are also very good at spotting a ringer from the get-go," Dr. Wren said, smiling. "That is what Jake says about you. Tell me, how are you able to spot a ringer from the get-go?" she inquired mischievously, taking a sip of warm highly acidic champagne.

It was not a big sip, and Mildred realized that the woman beside her was a kindred spirit. Mildred was also very good at taking small sips of drinks that were warm when they should be cold.

"So, do you have a strategy? Tips about how to spot a ringer?" Dr. Wren pressed. She set her flute down on the small table nearby.

"You are really asking me, aren't you?" Mildred confirmed, surprised. She took a stalling sip of warm champagne.

"Do you see a ringer in the room?" Dr. Wren asked, meeting Mildred's eyes fearlessly.

"I haven't been looking," Mildred said.

"I have been fooled a few times by ringers," Dr. Wren admitted easily. "When hiring personnel not being able to spot a ringer is an expensive mistake to make. It takes about six to seven years to get rid of a ringer once they are on board; and if they get tenure, make that twenty-five to life. Sounds like a prison sentence," Dr. Wren said. "If you were on our hiring committees, you could save the university a good deal of money and time if you can do it. Can you really spot a ringer?"

In any other environment, Mildred Budge would have feigned ignorance.

But the frank inquiry and fearless gaze caused Mildred Budge to tell the truth. "Yes. Sometimes I can."

"That is what Jake said you could do. How do you do it?"

Mildred repressed the uncomfortable idea that Jake had talked about her to anyone. In that moment, she did not have a list of traits she looked for in others.

"I pay attention to what I see. That's how I spot a ringer. Then, I believe what I see, no matter if mine is an unpopular opinion or not."

Dr. Wren held Mildred's gaze, her eyes searching to know what Mildred saw.

"How many are here in this room?" she asked finally.

Mildred's gaze swept the room slowly. There were many milling people making small talk. She couldn't hear anything of what was being said. But she watched their faces and how their bodies existed in space and with one another.

"Four," Mildred said finally with conviction. "The man at the door. Two women hovering near Jake. And that fellow at the end of the buffet table taking the cheese straws and fishing out the cashews in the nut bowl."

"How do you know?"

"The man at the door is holding it open as if he is a great friend to all, but he isn't. He fights the urge to slam it. The two women near Jake are not friends. They are competitors and staying close to keep an eye on the competition."

"They are competing for Jake," Dr. Wren observed. "He is popular with the ladies, and they may think this is their last chance to make a final play before he is out of their reach."

"He is already out of their reach. Jake doesn't even see them now. See?"

"I see," Dr. Wren concurred.

"The man in the uniform by the table is standing with four other members of the ROTC, but he isn't a team player. He is looking out for himself, gathering snacks for later. In war, he would leave you behind, or he wouldn't charge the enemy. Either way, you cannot rely on him."

"They are ringers," Dr. Wren confirmed.

"Or simply hypocrites, playing the social part they have assigned themselves. Sometimes that is the truth. But you have to look long enough, and you have to believe what you see. But when you do know, you have to believe that you know when you spot a ringer."

"You are referring to the little voices that come afterwards that cause us to second guess what we know by accusing us of bias, prejudice, or a lack of open-mindedness."

That response startled Mildred Budge who held universities and the people who work there with high esteem. "I thought being open minded was what a university is all about."

"We are as open minded as we can allow ourselves to be, but I suspect more of us can spot a ringer than we will admit to. Little voices yammering in judgment about the words we use to explain our point of view makes us doubt ourselves."

Mildred nodded, but an uncomfortable feeling took hold and her jaws tightened. The teeth of the plastic tortoise comb pushed down hard into her twisted knob of hair was biting into her scalp. "Jake doesn't know that I have been a ringer myself off and on through the years."

"That can't be true," Columbia said. "You can't be a ringer."

"Oh, yes it can. I am less of a ringer now than I have ever been, but I have been one off and for most of my life. Why there are mice running around loose?" Mildred asked, changing the subject. "And I mean no disrespect by asking," Mildred said, succumbing to the little voice that warned her that asking about unexpected guests, like mice, might offend someone somewhere somehow.

Dr. Wren's face grew stern. "People call it a prank."

"Students or professors?" Mildred asked.

"More often loose mice running around on campus is a professor's fault, and it is not a prank though that is what we all sort of collectively agree to say. Professors or their interns sometimes forget to lock the cages securely. And when that happens and the mice get out, they don't say they did it. They blame pranksters—students with a grudge about a grade or someone with a warped sense of humor. I don't like mice, and I don't think having them run around is funny. I do not like to have a mouse in my office or in the ladies' room. Sometimes they show up there at most inconvenient times."

It was a lengthy and honest confession that the vice president of the university did not allow herself to make to others.

Dr. Wren's attention was snagged by a woman who tapped on the podium and signaled that formalities were about to begin.

"I am going to have to say a few words. And the truth is, no one really wants to hear me make small talk about Jake retiring. They want to hear Jake Diamond play that piano," Dr. Wren said. "Maybe I will just trust what I know," she said, smiling to herself. "Mr. Diamond, are you just going to stand by that piano or are you going to do something about it?"

His eyes found the voice and Columbia, and then Jake saw that his boss was standing next to Mildred Budge. His eyes warmed.

"What do you want, Doctor?" he asked.

"Oh, just one of those things," she replied, cryptically.

Jake nodded that he understood, motioning to Chase to settle down beside him on the ebony piano bench.

Mildred Budge watched as one of the ladies rolled back the ornate tapestry to the back of the grand piano.

Jake lifted up the lid of the piano and tapped a few keys. The room quietened. Friends and ringers alike stopped, turned and paid attention.

"We keep the tapestry on it because people want to set drinks on it," Columbia explained. "Do you want to sit down?"

Mildred followed Columbia to a pair of wingback chairs near the door that led to the kitchen.

"Jake usually starts with Cole Porter. But he never plays any song the same way twice," she said, settling in. "The best part of any occasion," she remarked, letting herself relax.

Mildred swallowed hard, suddenly aware of the rolled-up pants at her waist. She looked down at her feet. She could see them. The pants were still rolled up. She patted the back of her hair, pressing on the tortoise shell comb again. It was holding. Chase was fine. Forty-five minutes had passed. *How long was a retirement party?*

"Magic time," Columbia said.

Mildred tucked one tired foot behind the other at the ankle, her hand smoothing the fabric of the taupe traveling pants. They didn't feel like hers. But they were hers. She wondered what else was in that closet. Shopping in a dead woman's closet was easier to do than driving to a dress shop in Georgia without directions, but did wearing her clothes make you a ringer of sorts?

"We are going to miss Jake's music. Even our music director can't do what Jake can do at the piano."

The music from the piano grew louder then and the people in the room gravitated toward Jake.

"Just one of those things," Columbia mused, retreating into her inner world where she experienced music. "He plays until the Lord shows up," Columbia said. "Or at least that is how he explained it to me. I think he must mean when beauty happens."

Mildred listened in silence and wonder. Time passed. Small talk wasn't necessary. Jake was a revelation. The mice left. Chase was beside him, paying attention.

The music slowed and worked toward its natural resolution, away from sound to the kind of silence that holds you close.

"I don't want the music to stop," Columbia said. "Because this is most likely the last time I will hear Jake Diamond play. Does he play at your church?"

Mildred shook her head. "We don't know about Jake's music at church." She eyed him curiously. He had never played the Baldwin Studio piano in her den either.

Clapping ensued, and people pressed in closer to Jake, who nudged Chase to find Mildred. Jake needed to make his good-byes. The boy stood, moving as easily as a white mouse among the well-wishers until he saw Mildred and walked directly to her.

Taking his place beside her, Mildred said, "Sweetheart, this is Dr. Wren. Jake's boss."

Slowly, slowly, Chase's gaze rotated over to the other woman who let her eyes smile for her.

"It was nice to meet you, Millie. Jake calls you that sometimes, too. I hope I see you again," Dr. Wren said, and Mildred believed her.

"Good-bye, Chase. I hope when you are ready to go to college, you will give us a chance," she said, reaching out for his hand. He took it, surprising Mildred again.

In that instant, Mildred felt the other woman's yearning to help the boy and what she must feel for all of the young people at the university growing up, learning, learning what they didn't want to be, learning what they wanted to know more about. Learning—what an adventure it is all your life long.

Seeing Dr. Wren tell Chase good-bye so warmly was the first occasion in a long while since Mildred had retired that she missed the feeling of protective nurturing of students finding their way toward their futures, an expansive domain that Dr. Wren still inhabited. "Jake will be with you in a moment. I will say a few words, and the people here will scatter like white mice," she predicted, her smile different now. She was looking into the future without Jake and she looked lonely.

Dr. Wren took the center of the room and said nice things about the contributions Jake had made to the university and how they would miss him, and before she finished her farewell remarks, various people in attendance drinking champagne and eating nibbles began to slip out one of the two doors, headed to teach a late afternoon class, headed home for a shower and supper, headed to working more years, headed away from yesterday's news: *Jake Diamond retired. Yes, he did. Jake who?*

Jake spoke tenderly to Dr. Wren, holding her hand the whole time. And when he did let go, Mildred saw that it was hard for him to turn his back on her and walk away.

"The wonder years," Jake said, and he weaved slightly, the strain of taking his leave taking a toll. "Let's go home."

The party had been a great success.

Dr. Wren was smashing, wasn't she?

Oh, yes.

They are a great bunch of people.

Oh, yes.

Not a ringer in the bunch," Jake said, smiling as he drove, his hand holding the wheel easily, his eyes focused on the road and his future.

"No," Mildred agreed. "Not a ringer in the bunch," she agreed readily, and in that moment, Mildred felt a stab of remorse, for she regretted the small talk with Dr. Wren and how she had succumbed to the temptation to be a voice of omniscience about ringers that simply wasn't true. For Mildred Budge knew truly and from experience that if you looked long and kindly enough at anyone, no one was a ringer really. Some people were just more comfortable in themselves than other people are at parties and other places.

Dusk was falling. The parking lot lights were beginning to beam, casting that strange pallor on the dark asphalt and the parked cars.

"Did you get anything to eat?" Jake asked, his hand steering the Expedition out of his assigned parking spot for the last time, looking over his shoulder carefully.

Mildred remembered the last time she had left the parking lot of her old school. She had no regrets, but there was this longing from time to time to know how everyone was doing.

"I am fine," she said, peering out the window. She caught a glimpse of herself in the glass, her face one of repose. Her hair was still up, and she had cheekbones again. Seeing herself, Mildred Budge smiled. In the shadows, in the moonlight, she was almost a girl again out on a date and driving home in the dark.

"Chase?"

The boy didn't immediately answer. He, too, was staring out the window thinking his own thoughts.

"It is early," Jake said. "And I didn't eat. How about we go to the Dairy Queen and have hamburgers and milk shakes?"

"And French fries?" Chase asked, straining forward from the back seat to join in the conversation.

"You betcha!" Jake affirmed.

She turned and looked directly and closely into the little boy's eyes.

In that moment, they were brimming with appetite and curiosity. He was close to the surface where everyone lived. He was hers. And he was Jake's. And he was Fran's and Winston's, too.

"The Dairy Queen sounds good!" she agreed. "Let's go."

13

GOT A MINUTE?

"See you, little fella," Jake said, patting Chase on the right shoulder.

The boy was tired and went on inside the house ahead of them.

"I will be along. Can you get ready for bed?" Mildred called after him.

Chase didn't answer her-- just kept walking toward his room.

Mildred and Jake waited for the boy to reach the end of the hallway and then turned to say their good-nights.

"Got a minute, Millie?" Jake asked.

Mildred nodded. She had a minute.

"Do I owe you an apology?" Jake asked abruptly.

Standing in the foyer, he looked around restlessly as if he were seeing it for the first time, and he was now from the perspective of a retired person.

The world looks different after you retire.

"I can't think of anything you should be sorry for," Mildred replied honestly. She looked longingly at the sofa. Her feet hurt. Her head itched. She wanted a shower.

"Could we sit down a minute?" Jake asked, but he didn't move toward the sofa in the living room. Instead, he pointed toward the back of the house. "How about the sun porch? It is farther away from listening ears."

"Do you want coffee?" she offered automatically as they passed through the kitchen. No one she knew drank coffee this time of night.

Jake was no different. "Too late for me, Millie."

It was too late for her to drink caffeine too; but Jake had just retired, and he seemed to want to talk. He probably had a lot on his mind. Sometimes, holding a cup of something warm helped you say what you had on your mind.

At the doorway that led from the kitchen into the sun porch, Mildred automatically reached out for the light switch.

"We don't need it," Jake said, his hand going out and covering hers over the light switch, stopping her from turning on the light.

Her foot hesitated, staying in the air before she planted it on the brick flooring, her attention coming to the fore. In the shadows, trusting muscle memory to guide her, Mildred's right hand reached out to find the back of the wicker chair and maintain her balance.

That chair was all the real space she had left in the house that was her own—her breathing room. And now Jake was filling up the last space she had.

Settling into her Bible-reading chair, Mildred espied her steno pad with the morning outline for the Sunday school lesson stuffed awkwardly in the wooden magazine rack.

She sat up straighter, her hand fidgeting with the comb holding her hair. She was eager to take it out, brush out her hair, and wash her face. All the smiling at the party had made her facial muscles tired. Perhaps they could just get to Jake's point sooner. "Whatever it was that you think requires an apology, don't worry about it. I can't think of anything you have ever done that has bothered me."

Sitting across from her, Jake leaned forward and took both her hands and held them in his. "Mildred Budge, you make loving others look easy."

Her body tensed immediately. "I am not..." she began, but before she could continue her thought he rushed in with what he had been wanting to say for a long time.

"Whether you know it or not, I do owe you an apology, Mildred. I used you at the party today."

"I don't understand," she said, truthfully.

"I wanted you there at the party today to signal to those two women at the piano that I wasn't available the way they want me to be. The way I have been, Millie, if I am being honest, and I want to be honest with you. You didn't know that about me, did you?"

Jake didn't expect an answer, so Mildred did not give him one. She waited to let him speak. He was intent on doing just that.

"I sent those two women on their merry way by implying that I was with you, and that means I used you."

She stopped herself from saying, 'I was with you. We went to a party. You didn't want to go alone.'

"Mildred, you only know me from church. But at the university I have—had." Jake shrugged, trying to make himself clear, and she marveled that she had never seen him not in charge of himself.

"I like the ladies; and the truth is, ladies like me. Most ladies anyway," he said with a self-effacing grin.

He focused his attention on her—willing her to understand.

She stifled an unladylike yawn, the day catching up with her. The dead lady's pants she was wearing had stretched out and felt uncomfortably looser. That was an unusual feeling for her. Her clothes tended to feel too tight after a while—not looser. She liked the dead woman. She was going to look harder in that closet. Tomorrow, she was going to wash what she was wearing on the delicate cycle and hang them out to dry. She believed she could wear this outfit to church.

"Mildred. Mildred," Jake repeated her name. "Are you with me?" he asked. And in the hearing of it she also heard Fran snap her fingers twice. *Attention. Attention.*

"I am here," she said. Mildred returned to the present moment, letting the sound of Jake's voice reach her and draw her back to what he had on his mind and needed to say. "I am listening. Of course you have friends."

"Mildred, I like women," Jake added with a short laugh.

"You like everybody," she replied easily.

"There you go, Mildred. You thought I like everybody, because you like everybody. But not everybody likes everybody else and goes to a party to keep them company, because that is what you thought you were doing."

"Fran usually keeps me company at parties. She makes the small talk," Mildred offered. "I was going to try to do that for you if you needed me to. Sometimes, we need someone to do that for us."

"To run interference," Jake conceded. "So, you thought you were there to help me with small talk? To run interference?" He settled back, a rueful smile on his face.

"So maybe I don't owe you an apology, because what I needed was for you to run interference, and you just said you knew you were doing that."

She felt him study her in the shadowy room, searching for an answer. She had none to give him.

"Those two women hanging around me saw that I was there with you, and maybe they will stop calling me and texting me with stopped-up drains and lawn mowers that won't crank and anything else that is a problem they think I can solve for them."

It was the first time Jake had ever complained in her presence. She came to full attention.

"Their problems aren't real. They are a ruse, Mildred. They call me to help them, but they want something else; and I wanted you to help me solve that problem. I used you that way," he confessed.

He leaned back in his chair and crossed one leg over the other, a move her daddy used to make and which Mildred did too sometimes when her hip joint needed relaxing. It wasn't a ladylike way to sit, but she sat like that sometimes, too.

"I don't think you used me. I think you relied upon me. We are friends. We can rely on one another. I rely on you, and I don't even need to ask you. Somehow you always seem to know what I need, and you are always reliably there. I don't thank you enough for that."

Jake waved away the offer of gratitude.

"We are way past that, Mildred."

"Are we?" she asked.

"I am different now, Mildred. Ever since we went over that embankment, and you said, 'Jesus saves' I haven't been the same man. I don't need the ladies calling me, and I don't need your gratitude for the ways that I take from you that looks like I am helping you. I thought you already knew that." He studied her with surprise.

She smiled at him in the shadows.

Across the field Belle's kitchen light came on. Mildred could almost see her friend working at her kitchen sink, tidying up before going to bed. Jake was still talking. She wanted to get out of the dead lady's clothes. She needed to go check on Chase. How was Janie? Tomorrow her best friend was going in for a biopsy.

She confronted Jake and said firmly, sitting up taller in her chair, a signal that they could both go on, he to his house and she to her bed. "We are all right, Jake. Aren't we all right?"

He didn't read any of her signals.

"You said those words—Jesus saves--when we were about to crash," he reminded her.

That drive with Sam and Belle over the embankment was a while ago. Mildred couldn't even remember how long ago it was. She just knew that a lot had happened since then.

"Jesus saves," Mildred replied, companionably.

There was an old hymn with that in it, wasn't there? The Bereans would enjoy singing that hymn. Mildred couldn't think of the tune, but she had several hymnals and could track it down. She started humming to herself, to store the phrase and solve the mystery of it in the morning.

"Mildred? Mildred?" Jake repeated her name the way that Fran snapped her fingers.

"I am here," she assured him. She inhaled deeply and exhaled slowly, not a sigh. She was coming back to the moment.

He eyed her quizzically, suddenly standing up as if he were going to leave. "This is your room," he stated. "It is where you are," he affirmed.

"Mostly," she said, taking a breath. No single room in the house was all her own anymore--inviolate. Sooner or later someone came into any room where she was. She heard movement in the other part of the house. Janie or Chase. Chase needed to go to bed. Janie needed to get out of it. She wanted to go in her room, close the door, kneel down by her bed, and groan her evening prayer.

"I know you have got a full house and lots of people to cook for and a Sunday school class where you teach a lesson every so often,"

"Once a month," she said, glad she had some information that was easy to say. "I teach a lesson once a month." And she suddenly remembered her lesson idea from the morning, and she smiled. *Oh, yes. Jesus saves. Oh, yes. And he does it with a smile.*

"I want you to be sign up for a mission trip. We need you, Mildred. If you would sign up, other ladies would follow your lead. You have a lot of influence at church, and I am asking you to use it."

"I don't want to do that," she replied plainly.

He didn't hear her.

"Even though I was going to church, I didn't know Jesus saves for the longest time; and now I do, and we have got to tell other people in as many ways as we can, and that means we need to go on mission trips."

"Does it?" she asked.

"You don't think so?" he asked, settling back down.

"I don't think about it very much," she replied.

He was just barely retired and already filling up his calendar. He had yet to learn that an empty calendar could be arranged differently. Life could be lived differently.

"If you were with us on the mission trip," he began. "Other ladies would understand that we are on a mission trip. We would be together, but we would be working together."

"You want me to run interference on the mission trip," she concluded.

Ah. He didn't so much want her on the trip as he was afraid of himself being on the trip without her and with the other ladies who might sign up just to be closer to him. He was a ladies' man in a way that Mark wasn't.

It was late and a mission trip didn't feel like her problem. She considered the question. "I'll think about it," she said.

"You'll think about it?" he confirmed gladly. "And the boy can come. It would be good for him too. He hasn't seen much of the world."

"I'll think about it," she confirmed. That sentence was a code phase for *I'll pray about it*, which is what she meant. But she wouldn't be praying about going on the trip. She would be praying about how to tell Jake she wasn't going.

"That's just right. Just right," he agreed, finally making a move to leave. "That car you gave the boy and me...it's a classic. I wanted to have it ready for today and take you and Chase to the university in it. That was my big idea. I wanted to drive it over here and take us to the retirement party in the Mercedes, but I couldn't make it happen. We couldn't get it fixed in time."

"Things often take longer than you expect," she soothed.

People fretted so about so many things. She had not expected for Jake to worry over something like this.

"The Deerborns are still up," he announced suddenly.

"Belle likes to work her crossword puzzles after Sam settles down."

"What is your next lesson on?" he asked. "I have never heard you teach Sunday school. They won't let us go to the women's only Berean class. Pure discrimination against men. I might crash your class the day you teach. What are they going to do to me?"

"You can come anytime you want to," she invited. Mildred didn't add the church ladies' credo that guided them throughout their lifetime of service: *Don't ask permission. Do what needs to be done, and if it breaks a rule, ask for forgiveness later.* People have to forgive your trespasses. It is in the Bible.

Jake preceded her out of the sun porch and waited in the kitchen, turning.

"My lesson is about those times in the Bible when Jesus smiled."

He didn't hear her. "You are going to be thinking about that mission trip," he repeated.

"Yes," Mildred agreed, and she felt such compassion for Jake who had not yet learned that retirement meant something different to her than it did to him.

"And you forgive me for using you today?" Jake asked, though he knew that it was unnecessary. He was practicing saying he was sorry after a lifetime of not doing that for so long in his life with so many other women.

"There is nothing to forgive," she replied easily.

And Jake leaned forward and kissed her on the lips, light and firm and affectionate—a man who has had a lot of lady friends and thinks nothing of kissing a woman good-night. It had been a while since a man had kissed her. The experience of physical affection was jarring for her but commonplace for him.

"I will see you soon, Millie," he said, but he was promising that to himself. "Why don't you go to bed? You are probably tired."

"That is a good idea," she said, closing the door after him. And as he walked away, she moaned, "Lord have mercy."

Mildred checked the lock, went to the kitchen to make the coffee pot for the next morning—sniffing the tap water, it was all right-- and stopped at Chase's room. He had put himself to bed, still wearing the clothes from the day.

Mildred felt a twinge of discomfort that she had not helped him. She draped a blanket over him and closed his door. She might do the same thing when she got in her room, just fall onto the bed and sleep in her clothes.

But she did not make it to her bedroom.

14

JUST ME ALONE

The girl was moaning, maybe crying. It was hard to tell what the sounds meant through the closed door.

Though rejected many times before, Mildred couldn't not ask if the girl needed help. She tapped on the bedroom door.

Then, she knocked again.

"Are you all right?" Mildred asked softly, but insistently.

Janie opened the door grudgingly. Behind her, the bed was a rumpled mess. The bassinette ready for the arrival of Little Mister was covered in dirty clothes tossed and piled there rather than washed and stored in the closet that Mildred had emptied out for her.

The disorder caused Mildred concern, but she tried not to let that worry show up in her eyes.

"There you are," Mildred confirmed. "I am just letting you know that I am back. Are you all right?"

"Why wouldn't I be all right?" Janie snapped. She removed one white ear bud and held it. "I called my social worker while you were out with your boyfriend."

"I didn't know you had a social worker," Mildred admitted.

Janie drew back, her voice growing louder in self-defense though Mildred had not accused her of anything. "I told you about Adelaide before, but you couldn't hear me. I have a social worker, and she is the one who is helping me."

"I didn't hear you," Mildred admitted.

She had actually heard Janie say something like that, but Mildred had thought the girl had meant someone like a parole officer. But, no, Janie had said social worker, and it was becoming clear in that moment, that social worker is what Janie had meant.

Janie nodded, irritably. "We have been talking," she explained, her chin jutting upward, her eyes red-rimmed and bloodshot. "There is no point in me not telling you. I am going to give up the baby. When this whole mess is over with, I can leave here, and you can have your house back. The boy will have you to himself, and Jake won't have to look at me like he does, and I will just go on. I will just go on," she vowed, looking past Mildred toward the hallway that led to the front door and her escape into a future that she could not see yet.

"If I leave, you won't have to move us all into that other house you bought. Just let me get through this, and I will go on and you can go on and we will all just go on."

Mildred wobbled. The muscles in her neck seized up, signaling an encroaching headache.

Janie waited for Mildred to say exactly the right thing.

"I didn't know Jake looked at you in a certain way. How does Jake look at you?" Mildred asked. He hadn't been around enough to see Janie—not inside the house anyway when she was out of her room.

"Like he feels sorry for me. He brought that glider over from Pastor Steev's backyard. Both of them toted it, and he said I could rock the baby in it outside in the sunshine, and he looked like he felt sorry for me. And I didn't like the way he looked at me. What business is it of his how I rock a baby?" She took a breath. "When I am gone you can get rid of that glider. Take it back over to that preacher's backyard. I don't need his cast-offs."

Mildred fought the urge to give way--to fall to the floor and go dormant.

She had heard about other women giving way like that. When it happened, someone usually reported afterwards as part of the news in the prayer chain: *She fell.*

And later, the woman who fell would explain as best she could: "My leg seemed to go weak. A muscle spasmed. I must have had vertigo."

Yes, let us call that kind of fall the result of vertigo. That answer was closer to the truth. Heartbreak hurts your ears, and you have inner ear trouble. Then, the heartbreak sinks in, and you sink, too.

Many reasons occur that cause otherwise stable church ladies to fall, but heartbreak was behind a lot of it.

A prayer from the deep well of her spirit coursed up through Mildred and trembled petitions. *God bless the world. God bless Janie. God bless the boy.* And just as her inner Mildred Budge was catching her breath, the sun porch door opened—how had she forgotten to check it? -- and she heard Sam call out from the kitchen.

"Millie-boo! Millie-boo! Where you are?" It was Sam's old voice he was using--this current version of Sam who was still roaming about, restlessly visiting his friends even after sundown. Belle would be looking for him, wondering. Millie would have to call Belle or take Sam home herself.

"Millie-boo! Where are you?" he repeated his question, coming toward them both. And his greeting stopped Mildred Budge from succumbing to heartbreak and gravity.

But he didn't know that, and no one listening or watching could have known that in that moment the old man with dementia who was making his rounds was also a hero of sorts—just a different kind than people recognize and celebrate with praise. When someone with dementia does a good turn, most people don't see it.

Sam found his friend Mildred Budge standing in the shadowy hallway with Janie lodged in the doorway of her bedroom.

"Girly-o," Sam called out happily. "Millie-boo!" He repeated, smiling broadly as if coming into her house and roaming about was perfectly natural. And it was for Sam.

Mildred thought instantly of moving to the new house and how Sam would not know how to find her right away though he knew the house. He would not come through the back door of the other house so easily for there was no muscle memory to guide him there. In a different location that was only a few blocks away, Sam would still not immediately know where she was, and neither would Belle. There would be no pathways of years of friendship to help Sam find his way to the safe place called Mildred's house.

Her hand reached out and found balance by touching the wall. That was the same activity that Sam was doing. He was touching base; and if she moved away, Sam would miss her here. *Yes, he would.* Mildred choked back a sob of loss that she rarely allowed herself to acknowledge as real. She grieved for the ways she was losing Sam to his disease.

"Fat girl!" he exclaimed, seeing Janie. "How did you get so fat?" he asked Janie.

Before she tried to answer or slam the bedroom door in his face, Sam turned and studied Mildred. "You look so pretty tonight. Why so blue, Millie-boo?" Sam asked, and he kissed her suddenly and loudly on the side of her face near her ear, making a loud boisterous sound and causing her to want to cover that noise-afflicted ear with her hand, but she didn't.

It was Mildred's second kiss of the evening, but who was counting? She was still in danger of falling, her shoulders rounding into what could become a stoop associated with old age if she didn't hold herself up and her shoulders back.

Using Sam's presence as an opportunity to escape, Janie stepped back into her room, and started to push the door closed. Like an old-fashioned door-to-door salesman, Mildred shifted her foot to keep the door from being completely closed. She was not going to let the girl be alone. Not that alone. Raising one finger in a way that she did not raise it very often anymore, she signaled, *Hold on. We're not through yet.*

"Millie-boo," Sam said, consolingly. "You worry too much."

Mildred rubbed the place between her brows where tension knotted.

"Did you want to say something else?"

Janie turned toward the bed, which was rumpled, the tumbled mess of blankets and sheets so unwelcoming. She never made it, because she didn't get out of it for long.

"The phone rang then, and Mildred ignored it. People shouldn't call after eight o'clock at night.

"You always do that," Janie accused.

"Do what?" Mildred demanded, her foot beginning to feel the pain of blocking the door from closing.

"You don't answer the phone when you are talking to someone else." Janie's eyes searched Mildred Budge's face for an answer to such a mystery.

"I am talking to you right now about Little Mister. That person can leave a message," Mildred explained. Her foot spasmed from the pressure of the door, and she finally wrenched it back.

Janie slammed the door and cried out, "Don't ever call the fetus that name again. Oh, why don't you just leave me alone?

DAY 2

The Lord is near to all who call upon Him,
to all who call upon Him in truth.
He will fulfill the desire of those who fear Him;
He also will hear their cry and save them.

Psalm 145: 18-19

1 5

HUMANTIME

The day after Fran Holmes told Mildred Budge that she had a lump-thing, Mildred Budge faced morning time differently than she had the day before.

Mildred woke up in her own house. She poured her own coffee. She carried the cup to the back porch and settled down, ignoring the memory of Jake in the chair nearby from the night before. In a way he was still there, but she didn't address that echo in time that some people referred to less precisely as a memory.

Instead, good neighbor Mildred Budge stood and surveyed her back field until her gaze settled on the Deerborns' house. Once she confirmed that everything seemed all right out there, Fran's and Sam's and Janie's and Belle's best friend submitted to the moment of ordained morning time.

Growing disciplined day after day, the church lady waited until the truth moved up in her and enabled her to speak love in the creative act people refer to cavalierly as prayer.

Moving toward that moment of truth felt at times like you were in a jungle of worry and concerns and pushing through the overgrowth of dread and fear until you reached a clearing where the sunlight falls through everything that is incessantly yammering for your attention; and in a moment of bliss that was only yesterday called joy, the sweet silence of rest covers you.

The light from this sweet silence of rest dispels dread, worry, and fear, and you can hear with a faculty loosely pointed to as faith what could be whispered from the deepest part of yourself to God and be assured that something bigger than yourself is united to the Way that is promised in the Bible, and that Way is the Bridegroom of the Strong Tower who loves Fran more than Winston does or could—more than Mildred loves her best friend, too.

It always surprised Mildred to remember that God loves everyone she loved more than she did or ever could.

And it was that love of His for everyone she loved that Mildred Budge sought through the jungle and clamor of worry; and when she found it, the experience of time changed. Again.

The church lady moved into that dimension called eternity; and, it, like the word faith, has a phrase of its own that does not tell the whole truth. That place where prayer intersects with eternity can be called a thin place or kingdom-come time, and no hand on a clock or even a beat of the human heart explains that experience of time. It happens, and it is real, like Jesus and the stories about him in his biography, the Bible.

Mildred trusted the experience of kingdom-come time. Followers of Jesus often do, and though they proclaim the intersection with holiness in cliches and messages on bumper stickers, inside every living, lit-up person who knows kingdom-come time there is a solemnity born of irresistible devotion to Love itself.

Loving Love is not a virtue. It is inevitable, like joy. Infusing the solemnity of union with Christ is a potent joy that lifts you up and accompanies you into the next moment and the moment after that with an appetite to be fully alive and grateful—so grateful.

Kingdom-come prayers wake up with you.

Kingdom-come prayers always give way to joy, no matter what the circumstances, if you let them.

Kingdom-come living is a safe place to love others without the fear of falling down from devastating heartbreak.

And so, while Mildred Budge sipped her morning coffee automatically, those physical senses in her that had preferences for warmth and cold, soft and not as soft, this and that receded into a dormant space inside of her that opened up by letting go.

Time passed in all kinds of ways. She hummed. Angels sang along. Her attention shifted. As lights came on across the open field at the Deerborns's house, Mildred Budge began to sort out the tasks in front of her friend Fran, beginning with the biopsy, the reader of the biopsy, the doctor who would manage the sequence of steps called cancer care if that was the case, and then the prospect of chemotherapy or radiation and what else could follow that the church lady didn't know about. There was more to praying about cancer than knowing the facts of it or the steps of protocol in treating it.

And then, Mildred prayed for the baby that she was not allowed by his mother now to call Little Mister, and so she didn't say his name except to God. She asked Him to write the child's name down in the Book of Life wherever the child lived out his days.

And she held up Chase and the way he spent his time, and she thanked God for the growing glint in his young eyes and for Jake teaching him to say dip stick and gizmo and for creating that occasion when you learn that too much mustard on a bologna sandwich is too much mustard and the only way to know that is to experience it.

And she prayed for Jake and how he was meant to live in Jesus saves as a retired man who was renovating an old car and teaching a young boy how to work with his hands.

And she prayed for the Jesus Saves committee and the work and words, and she hoped Jake wouldn't call on her to pray in public, because she didn't like to pray in public. It wasn't because she was shy. It was because prayers could become so very impolite, crossing boundaries of good behavior. And sometimes they could get very loud when your love surged up and forth in kingdom-come time. At home, Mildred did not quench those prayers; in public, she felt self-conscious about loving others so loudly and without restraint.

Life was too short to pray politely with others; and in that moment, she prayed that she could live up to that ideal that prayers should never devolve into small talk.

While she was praying impolitely for Janie and the baby, someone out there was praying they could have a baby, and Mildred felt like she was in the middle, praying for what would be best for everyone and that always led her to "thy kingdom come thy, will be done." That benediction covered quite a lot of need and every condition of the human heart. *Yes, it did.*

She held up Janie to the Light of Love and said, "I do not know what to do about her. She has locked herself away. Made herself a prisoner. How do you want to go about setting her free?"

And after that confession of ignorance as blissfully and gratefully uttered as a confession of sin, Mildred twisted her head from side to side, reminding herself that being relaxed was not a sin and that you can have a better-feeling body if you take the time to name every anxiety you have by casting them upon the One who cares for you, and that includes the great confession that you are not as smart as you wish you were and sometimes others expect you to be, and you can be as old as anything and not be smart enough to answer questions about a young woman with a baby coming and a young boy who was doing so much better than anyone could have predicted, praise the Lord.

The ascription of praise came easily and was familiar, for when she began to praise the Lord, Mildred Budge sensed with her spirit that she was coming to a temporary end of that morning's prayer time. Life inside her house was waking up, and soon Chase would need his breakfast and Janie would come out when Mildred left to go tag furniture at the new house to be sent on to The Emporium.

Rising, Mildred Budge turned toward the kitchen. Chase was standing in the doorway in the same clothes he had worn the day before, but now he was holding something in his hands.

He came into focus slowly, and as the details of his appearance told the story that she had lost the battle last night to get him changed and he didn't have an appointment for the dentist yet and she wasn't sure what he had clean to wear today, she took a breath and postponed the taking on of that guilt and the to-do list and seemed to be always hovering, hovering. She asked instead, "Chase, what have you got there?"

He didn't answer her, just stepped forward from the shadows into the morning light coming in through the windows.

She recognized the model car from the kit Winston and Fran had brought him from their honeymoon. "How did you do that? Could you read the instructions?"

"Only in English," he replied. "Janie snores," he reported, but it was not a complaint. He was just telling her something.

And then Chase went back to the kitchen to pour his own bowl of Cheerios.

16

LABOR PAINS

"The fetus is coming," Janie announced, standing in the doorway—leaning really.

She was wearing a man's extra-large white V-neck T-shirt and what appeared to be blue and white boxer shorts. Mildred had no idea where they had come from. Janie had come home from jail with one big suitcase holding the personal items she had arrived with months before when she and Al, her significant other, had been houseguests of Mildred. They were probably Al's clothes, Mildred figured.

The mother-to-be in front of her looked even more surprised than Mildred felt, and she was in dire need of a robe. The girl's eyes were scared, her gaze hopeless.

"Just call me a taxi. I can go to the hospital alone. Somebody has got to stay with the boy. Cause I don't want that little goofball around. He talks to himself, mumbling up and down the hallway night and day."

Mildred filed that information away. The girl had been listening on the other side of the door, but it wasn't Chase she heard. Mildred paced and sometimes mumbled prayers while walking up and down the hallway.

"No one is going anywhere in a taxi and certainly not to the hospital. I need five minutes to get dressed," Mildred declared, the muscles across her chest constricting. Her shoulders tightened. She felt a headache begin.

Janie plopped down heavily in the chair at the kitchen table. "I don't want to do this."

She looked up at Mildred, and for a flicker of a second there was a vestige of the girl Mildred had met during the missions' conference. Young and vulnerable and searching for love and friendship.

"I will call Belle," Mildred said, blinking. Belle's lights were on; her neighbor was up.

"Call the social worker," Janie said. "She needs to bring the papers for me to sign and come get the fetus."

"Little Mister," Mildred whispered, her voice an echo of pain.

"No. He's a fetus," Janie objected.

Mildred flinched, dialing Belle's number. "It's Janie's time," she reported, her voice low and urgent.

"Coming," Belle replied, for long-time friends don't need as many words as others imagine.

"The back door is open."

"No worries," Belle said, the caregiver of a husband with Alzheimer's, and in that moment, she meant it.

It was Belle's signature good-bye now and different from the ones she used to make, which had been playful: *See ya, Babe.* Belle didn't call anyone *Babe* anymore, and she had stopped doing a little salsa sashay when she left a room.

Mildred missed the salsa sashay and the *good-bye, babe* in Belle in that moment. Where had the old Belle gone, and who is this new Belle with a houseful of trouble who promised readily and convincingly, *no worries?*

In the kitchen, Janie groaned and bent over.

"Put your arms through this," Mildred directed as she held out one of her robes from the hope chest reserved for time spent in a hospital. It was a deluxe sky-blue quilted satin robe.

Mildred's voice was cold, official—foreign to her own ears. "Can you slip your feet into these shoes?"

"My feet are swollen. Shoes don't fit now."

Oh.

"You need some slippers," Mildred concluded, hurrying back to the hope chest in her bedroom in which were stored two pairs of mink-trimmed, slide-on slippers, gifts from a former student who owned a string of high-end boutiques. She had sent Dear Miss Budge a pair of large slippers year before last and another pair the next year.

Janie stared at the slippers; her face drawn. And then she looked up at Mildred, her gaze questioning. *How did life get so hard?* But that is not what she asked. "Do you think I am going to die?"

Mildred held up one finger. "We are all right," Mildred promised. She should probably ask her how long the contractions had been happening and how much time was in between each one. But Mildred was afraid to ask. The answer might force her to move faster than she felt she could, and Mildred was already moving faster than was comfortable.

"Take deep breaths," Mildred advised, looking longingly at the telephone.

Fran was busy with her biopsy this morning, and when she had looked out the front window Steev's van was already gone. Mildred had pledged to herself that she would not keep tabs on Steev's comings and goings when the young preacher rented the house she owned across the street. *You live your life, preacherman. And I will live mine.*

Mildred hurried to her room and slipped on her Wal-Mart shopping pantsuit, the green one with elastic waist and a lightweight corduroy. Considered a winter fabric, Mildred wore the corduroy pantsuit year-round and especially to a hospital where the air conditioning was unpredictable. Like other women her age, Mildred feared being cold, and she couldn't remember when that fear had taken hold. *So, what if she got cold? Shivered? It didn't mean the end was coming.*

Mildred splashed some water on her face, grabbed her purse, realizing suddenly that her heart was racing. Pressing one open palm to her forehead, she felt warm, like she was starting to run a fever. This was no time to get sick.

"Not now, Lord," she prayed. "I don't need any more trouble today."

The back door of the porch opened, and Belle called out, "Why are you still here?"

"We are almost out the door," Mildred said.

"Sam woke up when the phone rang. I told my old boy to hold down the fort while I am over here," Belle reported, standing with both feet placed solidly on the floor.

"But I will hold it down. Do whatever you need to do. We are all right here for as long as it takes."

Belle looked like herself in that moment: staunch, ready, and stronger than she had ever been before.

Her heart racing too fast, Mildred stopped at Chase's room and explained, "Chase, Aunt Belle is here. You're with her and Uncle Sam today, and maybe Uncle Jake later if he comes over to work on the playhouse. But I will be back when I can get here."

Chase was fiddling with the model car again, doing something with the wheels.

"You are okay then," she said, leaning over and kissing the top of his head.

He stiffened momentarily, forgetting so soon that he was loved and safe. It takes time to remember that love can become a constant. As soon as she retreated, his hands got busy again.

For every goodbye to Chase, Mildred wanted to reassure him that she would not leave him forever—would never run off, the sound of her car's tires peeling at the corner in the haste to leave him. *Never. Never. Never.* Mildred waited to see if he was concerned, but all Chase said was, "Adios, amiga."

Who was teaching him Spanish?

She nodded to the back of his head and retreated into the hallway, returning to Belle in the kitchen. "Call Jake if you need anything, Belle. He is retired."

Mildred winced, hearing herself say those words. Those were the very words she had not wanted spoken about her when she retired. *Don't plan my life for me.*

Her purse on one arm and her other arm around the leaning, moaning Janie, Mildred told Belle, "Chase is still wearing yesterday's clothes."

"Story of my life," Belle replied easily. "No worries." It was her mantra now.

"I will let you know how things go when I can," Mildred said.

Belle's gaze was intent. She nodded and warned, "I might need to raid your fridge. I am almost out of bread, butter, and eggs. I haven't been able to get to the grocery store this week."

"I wish you would," Mildred replied honestly. She needed to winnow out the fridge and the freezer. Belle helping herself to anything she wanted would be a big help.

"There is a roast in there if you feel like fooling with it."

But she wasn't sure Belle heard her. Janie had started moaning again.

PARKING SPACE

In the car on the way to the hospital, Janie was clutching her belly, panting hard and fast, and saying words that Mildred Budge only heard on television because her church friends didn't cuss like that.

Mildred could feel her heartbeat pulsing in her neck. Her blood pressure felt high; her chest felt tight. Her whole being longed for quiet and the ease of prayerful contemplation as she steered her red and black mini-Cooper left toward the hospital awning to let Janie out in front of the sliding doors that led to Admission.

The engine idling, Mildred hurried around the car to help Janie stand.

"Lean on me," Mildred urged as she heard footsteps coming hurriedly. *Mercy. Mercy.* Mildred took heart at the sound of the hurrying footsteps. "Yes! This is an emergency," she breathed. "Come quickly."

A nurse or an orderly was coming to their aid.

Janie gripped her forearm and squeezed.

Mildred stifled a yelp from the pain of Janie's intense grip, and turned to see what kind of help for the both of them was coming from the hospital.

"It never rains but it pours," Fran said, her blue eyes lit with concern. "Both of us here on the same morning."

Fran's sudden appearance startled Mildred.

Fran nodded. *It's me. I'm here.*

And her best friend was wearing her going-to-the-doctor outfit, a washable two-piece bright blue pants set with a top that had sleeves which rolled up so they could take your blood pressure or give you a shot without removing your shirt. The whole outfit washed up pretty on the delicate cycle and dried in 20 minutes on cool temperature. Fran Holmes only wore clothes to the hospital that could be washed at the end of the day, like her hair. Neither Fran nor Mildred slept in a bed with hair that had been collecting germs at hospitals or doctor's offices. They washed it no matter what day of the week it was.

In the moment of seeing Fran, Janie let loose a stream of words that Fran had heard many times before. You don't volunteer with hospice for twenty years and stand watch at various bedsides in all kinds of homes all over Montgomery without hearing an expressive vocabulary of pain and angst.

"I am sorry," Mildred said, incongruously.

Apologizing was one of the rejoinders of Southern church ladies everywhere.

Fran's reply matched Mildred's apology.

"Bless her heart," she said, as the contraction eased, and Janie tried to straighten up.

The pain had bowed Janie over, and her skin was pale, her face blanched with misery. When she looked up there was stark terror in her eyes.

"I am dying," she moaned. Holding her stomach, Janie was staring at the hospital and shaking her head, *no*. She wouldn't make herself go inside. That would mean that what was happening was inescapably real.

"Winston is parking our truck," Fran explained, her voice neutral. "Janie, try to stand up. You can do it. We just need to get you inside. I don't know why somebody hasn't come out here with a wheelchair. That is what we need."

Fran peered anxiously behind her to see if anyone inside was paying attention to the drama unfolding right on their doorstep, the drive-thru for Admissions.

"There is a woman in labor out here!" Fran mouthed the words to the tinted glass of the closed door hoping someone inside at the front desk could read her lips, because they couldn't hear her.

Janie took a deep breath and studied Fran's face as if she didn't recognize her. Fran nodded reassuringly, first to Janie and then to Mildred, who was temporarily immobilized.

"I have got her Mildred," Fran promised. "You go park your car. They don't let you leave it here in the drop-off lane."

Mildred stared at Fran as if she didn't understand English.

"What are you doing here?" Mildred asked. "I thought you would be at the cancer center," Mildred said.

"No. The procedure happens here at the hospital as an outpatient. Didn't I tell you that?"

Mildred shook her head. "Maybe," she said.

"I am right where I am supposed to be," Fran said with a kind of wonder in her voice. A faint smile of recognition dawned on her face, and her eyes grew brighter. "It is just a little biopsy. A routine procedure. Like pulling a tooth, only it is not a tooth."

Fran waited to see if Mildred smiled, but Mildred didn't smile.

Janie whimpered.

"Sweetheart," Fran said. "If you can't walk, I can get someone to bring out a wheel chair, but Mildred will have to wait here with you while I go back inside. Want to get going now?"

Standing straighter, Janie wobbled in place, staring at the mink-trimmed slipper on her right foot that didn't want to get going. Fran's arm went around Janie immediately, "I have got you."

"Nobody's got me," Janie snapped. She launched herself toward the automatic sliding glass doors, holding her belly as she tried to enter without them. The mink-trimmed satin slippers scuffed with every step. Mildred's blue satin robe billowed around her.

Suddenly, Winston hollered from where he was standing beside his green pick-up truck. Mildred barely heard her name and squinted, seeing Winston standing in a packed parking lot. Winston waved and pointed to an empty parking space beside his truck.

He couldn't leave the valuable empty space to come tell her to hurry, so he was waving his arms and yelling, "Here! Here!" Finally, cupping his mouth Winston called out, "Come on!"

Mildred moved as if in a trance, leaving Janie with Fran and going back around the car and settling inside, not bothering to clasp the seatbelt for the hundred-yard drive to Winston and the precious parking spot he was saving for her.

Looking down, Mildred saw her purse on the floor board and didn't remember grabbing it on the way out the front door. She couldn't remember whether she had locked her front door when she left or turned off the coffee pot. She had done nothing that was part of her leave-the-house routine.

Hands gripping the steering wheel, she said, "I don't know what I am doing. I don't know anything."

And then, because Fran's Winston was holding the space for her, Mildred drove the car out from under the hospital's awning, swung gently left, and steered her car to where Winston was guarding the empty slot. She hated to be watched while she was parking her car.

Winston opened her door for her, stepping back to give her wiggle room to get out. She couldn't remember if she had washed her face or combed her hair. She tried to smile anyway.

"Having fun yet?" he asked drily, the gaze in his eyes soft and vulnerable. Winston didn't look like himself. Or maybe he did. Mildred had never seen Winston's early morning face.

"I don't have any idea what I am doing this morning," Mildred replied honestly.

"Welcome to the club," Winston replied, shutting her car door gently. He smiled tiredly, the boyish gaze disappearing just that quickly.

Instantly, fear and fatigue created that familiar expression of people who endure until they fall down.

"It will be all right," Mildred promised automatically.

"I kind of want more than all right, don't you?" he replied, uncharacteristically wordy for him.

And just with that simple statement, Fran's best friend saw Winston Holmes take hold. Winston Holmes took hold when he told the truth that life for him was about more than endurance. He wanted more, and he had just told her that about him.

It gave Mildred the courage to tell Fran's husband the truth. "I want more than that, too," she admitted boldly though in that moment she couldn't name a single desire of her heart other than she wanted to go home.

Her breathing grew easier. A breeze brought a refreshing hint of morning cool to her skin. Her legs moved by habit.

They walked across the parking lot back to the double doors in silence, Mildred walking a little faster than usual to keep up with Winston, who had long legs and was in a hurry to reach Fran. Once he saw Fran standing in the doorway, Winston never took his eyes off of her.

Fran met them with an update, her eyes brimming with information and bright with purpose. Of the three of them, Fran had the hardest part of the day ahead of her, but she looked the least flummoxed.

"They have taken our girl to the back in a wheel chair. Before they rolled her away, Janie had them call her social worker. She was very adamant, dragging her feet on the floor until someone promised to do it," Fran reported.

She grew solemn, her brow furrowing in a way that it never had when she talked about getting the biopsy or the consequences of a diagnosis of breast cancer. "I didn't know our girl had a social worker."

Mildred nodded automatically, looking around for a water fountain. She was parched. Anxiety made her thirsty. She licked her dry lips, searching for moisture.

Fran's voice grew serious. "Janie told me that she's giving up our Little Mister. She told me that exactly. I didn't know that. I had not even thought of it as a possibility."

Mildred nodded again. The desires of her heart were coming back to her. She wanted coffee. She wanted water. She wanted to know where the bathroom was. She wanted quiet. Stillness. To catch her breath and breathe her prayers. But instead, her lower lip was now bleeding from where she had bitten it. Her ears were ringing, as if her blood pressure was up and climbing.

"I didn't know about it before last night," Mildred said, as Fran moved closer to Winston.

It was time for them to go find the place Fran needed to be so that she could hear the person call her name for her procedure.

"We are supposed to go that way," Fran said pointing down the hallway to a set of double doors that the two old friends had never gone through before. "I think you're up on three. I could be wrong."

All around the hospital the two church ladies knew the double doors and the waiting rooms and where the most private and less frequently used restrooms were and where communal waiting room coffee pots and vending machines were located.

It was a terrible fork in the road for Mildred Budge, who was always at the side of her best friend whatever the trouble; but in that moment--that morning--Mildred Budge was the only guardian advocate for Janie, mother of Little Mister. She must persevere and go to the waiting room where Janie needed her healthcare advocate to be.

Inhaling deeply, Fran said, "Do we know who this social worker is and how long it could take for her to get here, because there is still time to talk to Janie, isn't there? The girl needs somebody to explain...." Fran's voice drifted off, and Mildred didn't know where her thoughts went in that moment.

"We better go along. We have signed in, and someone may be calling your name," Winston said, taking Fran's elbow. He smiled gently at Mildred, apologizing in his way for taking Fran away. "You can only do what you do," he said, and his words were an apology and a plea. "It is time to go."

"Yes. Go on," Mildred said, trying to smile. But her facial muscles weren't working very well, and she needed to lie down. They don't tell you when you are young that when you are older, you want to lie down at inconvenient times.

"Maybe the biopsy won't take long," Fran said, looking up at Winston. "And we could join you."

Winston pointed with his index finger toward the doors, their destination. Fran was the desire of his heart and his single-minded concern.

"You know doctors and how long things can take," Mildred replied. She reached out and pressed the elevator button. It was only when she was safely inside and the doors were closing that Fran and Winston waved small good-byes and said simultaneously, "It will be all right."

Everybody was saying that to everybody else these days. Surely not everyone could expect a happy ending.

18

SOCIAL WORK

On the third floor, Mildred stopped at the nurses' station to let them know she was waiting for Janie and to find out if she needed to do anything else. Mildred had a blank check in her wallet, a credit card with a high limit if that was necessary, and a good ballpoint pen in her purse if she needed to sign something. But she didn't.

Janie and her social worker had arranged everything.

Surprised and more than a little disoriented, Mildred went to the appointed waiting room, which was empty.

She had been in many a hospital waiting room but never alone before or at least not for long. One of the Bereans would usually show up sooner or later. And, sometimes, a preacher would appear too—but not so often.

The waiting room had been recently cleaned. There was no trash or left-over debris from take-out meals on the tables or in the chairs.

The water cooler in the corner was half full or half empty, depending on your perspective. A single flimsy white cone-shaped paper cup was poking out of the plastic cylinder that held the stack of fifty they came in.

Mildred had refilled the plastic cup dispenser at her old school more times than she could remember, always pouring herself a cup of water to start the day before heading to class down the long hallway that smelled of harsh disinfectant. She filled a cup of cool water and found a seat where she could keep an eye on the double doors that led to the back.

There was a TV hanging from the ceiling in the corner in the waiting room. The flickering image was on, but blessedly, someone had muted the sound. Mildred stared at it for a moment. The TV show was one of those home improvement programs where they make over a room from being old-fashioned to modern.

That program played in her dentist's office, too. At least it wasn't one of the news channels with images forthcoming that they warned you would be disturbing.

Mildred sat down across from the television screen and without anyone to hear her complain about a television being on everywhere you went, she watched half-heartedly the silent screen, reading the subtitles that still crawled across the bottom of the screen even though the sound was muted.

The emcee home decorator was dressed in fawn-colored knee-high boots with tassels, had long, layered, high-lighted hair, a small diamond chip on the side of her nose, and heavy garish make-up she didn't need. Underneath all that make-up was a pretty girl, but you couldn't see that naturally pretty girl very easily. She was earnestly explaining what was wrong with the living room. As she pointed out the unnecessary old-fashioned built-in bookshelves, the dated teal green sofa, the matching club chairs, Mildred thought: 'There's nothing wrong with a room that has been lived in and looks like it. Read your books, and keep it dusted.'

And then the decorator with overdrawn lips signaled for the muscle men to come in and get to work.

Two men wearing black pants and black T-shirts began to tote everything out of it, leaving the floorspace empty.

Leaning forward toward the camera, she confided conspiratorially to the viewers. "Now, we are going to get rid of that carpet and see what's hiding underneath."

The men in black went to work, tearing out the perfectly good carpet that had some years of wear left in it. The carpet was a thick weave and would feel comfy on bare feet.

The men's work of tearing out the carpet was edited and sped up for the viewer, flashing forward in triple-time. Within minutes, the offensive room was stripped, including those deluxe bookshelves.

"No one needs more than thirty books," the emcee decorator explained with authority. "More than that, and you've got clutter. You don't want to be a clutter-bug, do you?" she asked the camera, her round blue eyes wide and saucer-like.

Mildred's own eyes widened in horror. She was so very different from other people, especially people on TV. She gave up watching the program then.

Settling down, she looked around the room and wondered why there weren't other people waiting. She wondered how Chase was doing and if Belle had found the roast in her freezer. She had some potatoes in the bin that Belle could use. Everyone loved creamed potatoes.

Mildred was busy planning a possible supper menu for Belle when the door opened again, and there he was: her neighbor, her tenant, her pastor. But she had not called Steev the pastor to come and wait with her.

"Belle phoned me," Steev explained, joining her. He sat down heavily; the youthful vigor of his step not present in the early morning hospital visit. "I let Jake know what was happening. He will go relieve Belle with Chase and then Sam will be all right. All the bases are covered," Steev assured Mildred, as she watched him pat her left knee reassuringly and then take away his hand.

His was still a youthful hand, though his knuckles were red, and the skin on his palms was rough from yardwork.

Settling back in his chair, Steev crossed one leg atop the other and commenced to make small talk. "Do you know when I go into a hospital now I check for exits and escape routes? Healthcare workers are often on the front line of a kind of violence that we still don't understand. Anyway, that is what I do now in hospitals and lots of other places. I look for the best escape route. If trouble happens, stick with me, kid. I will get us out of here," he promised.

"I will," she agreed automatically, wondering if Steev knew where the service elevator was and how exiting through it deposited you closer to the parking lot where she and Winston had left their vehicles to bake in the sun. Mildred didn't actively look for emergency exits because she already knew where most of them were.

"Are you getting enough sleep?" Mildred asked.

"Is anybody?" Steev replied tiredly.

'Well, yes,' she thought. 'I slept well last night.' But when she looked ahead toward the end of the day in front of her she did not have a prediction for the night. There was a reason a preacher didn't sleep well. He was either making congregational care calls, or someone or something was bothering him.

"Anyone giving you a hard time?" she asked delicately while staring straight ahead. It was a question Mildred had wanted to ask him for a long time. Steev had grown silent, distanced with her and she didn't know why. She suspected that he was seeing her as part of *them* now: the people in the congregation who were finding fault with him. It always happened. People love a preacher until they don't, no matter what the Bible says about love. They use some snippet of a verse from the Bible to justify their negative judgment, comfortable in wearing him down rather than building him up.

Steev turned to face her. "Now why would anybody give me a hard time?" he asked tiredly. "Did you know I received a petition from several members of the congregation who want me to change how I spell my name? They don't like the two e's in the middle. Apparently, it reflects badly on a church to have a preacher whose name looks like it is misspelled."

Mildred had heard more than one comment about that herself and had not paid much attention to it. Lots of rumbling went on most of the time in a church. Some of it had to do with sin; other times, it was about how you spell a name or something like that.

"I haven't decided what to do about it. I think it is triggering an identity crisis in me," he said, cutting his eyes at her to see if she could tell he was teasing.

She let her eyes smile back. "It is awfully hard to hold onto our identities when we are supposed to be getting sanctified," she added. "I don't even recognize myself in the mirror sometimes."

"I am supposed to still be in my honeymoon period as the new preacher in the church. Right now, and for a little while longer, the rumor is supposed to be that I can do no wrong, and everybody loves me."

Mildred immediately thought of Fran's honeymoon cut short, and her shoulders slumped, giving way as the cares of the world accumulated even when you believed in walking on water over the day's troubles with your feet shod with the promises of the gospel.

"If you don't think about it, it won't bother you," Mildred advised. "Willed forgetting is hard, but it can be done."

It is what she told church ladies to do when someone gave them a hard time. And people did. The hard times given to church ladies were different than the hard times given to youngish preachers who were still enthusiastic about the good news, she imagined. Over time, preachers and church ladies alike are supposed to wind down into a kind of somnolent maturity that is inoffensive.

"I like your idea better than turn the other cheek," Steev said. "I am getting whiplash from that one."

And just as he was talking about turning the other cheek, he turned his head to see who had just come through the door.

NO TIME TO WAIT

"She wouldn't listen to reason," Winston explained ruefully.

"I can listen to reason," Fran objected. "Only this is more reasonable," Fran argued. "Now, don't you worry, darlin'. They are rebooking my biopsy for next Friday. And if someone cancels, she promised to call me in. I told her I could get there lickety-split."

Mildred's head jerked with the words lickety-split. It felt all of a sudden as if Fran was using that phrase all the time now. Or at least, Fran had used it yesterday, and now she was saying it again. Time was flying for Fran because of the possible, imminent setback called cancer, and she wanted to move fast. Lickety-split.

"Another week doesn't matter. Time flies. You know it does. This morning, I am needed here more," Fran stated clearly, her blue-eyed gaze unconflicted. "What a cold room," Fran observed, stifling a shiver. "And so empty. Nobody else is having a baby?"

The words were no sooner out of her mouth than the opening strains of Brahms's Lullaby played over the loud speaker.

"They do that when a baby is born," Fran said. She shrugged. "I guess the people waiting for that baby are somewhere else." She stifled a shiver and looked around for a thermostat. She didn't see one. She saw the TV instead.

"At least the sound is turned off," Mildred said.

"That is something," Fran agreed, settling down on the chair on the other side of Mildred.

Winston steered Steev across the room to explain why they were there. Fran had not wanted anyone to know about the biopsy. Fran's problem wasn't a secret, but the process of solving the problem was private, for now. Fran never called the church to post any kind of prayer request, but Winston saw opportunity in Steev the preacher. He had cornered him and was talking low and fast.

"You know what I like about my husband?" Fran asked, her gaze growing gentle as she watched Winston talk intensely with Steev.

Mildred waited.

"He won't tell me later that having the preacher here was a divine appointment. It could very well be, but Winston won't say that. I like that about my husband."

"I like that about him, too," Mildred said, for she had a keen sense that one didn't assign the meaning of every day's moments to God not because He wasn't in charge but because life flowed, and human understanding of how it flowed was severely limited. Mildred rarely believed she knew exactly what was happening most days. She just trusted the motion of grace.

"Winston is not exactly mad at me," Fran explained, stretching out both legs. She crossed them at the ankle, one white Ked tipping against the other. Dark smudges on the toes and sides were showing through the white polish she had tried to use to hide the smudges that she had accrued in The Emporium's parking lot the day before. She had chosen a lickety-split cover up over a thorough cleaning with *Spic and Span*. Both women saw the stain coming through, and swapped knowing glances.

"I was in a hurry," Fran explained, her head shaking with resignation. "And now I am going to have to try soaking them in bleach. That won't work, but I will talk myself into trying it anyway." Fran shrugged and leaned back in the chair, letting her legs relax, her arms draped across her chest self protectively.

"I am finding out that when Winston seems peeved, he is really more scared than angry or upset. He sounds peeved, but he is really scared about this," she confided as Steev finished his conversation with Winston and then walked over to the double doors, pressed a small black button on the wall, and talked through the intercom with someone on the other side.

"I am not scared. I am the one who is actually peeved. Cancer irritates me. It is such an inconvenience."

Steev looked up at a camera aimed at the spot where he was standing and waved. Then, he pointed to a small gold cross on his collared golf shirt. Steev didn't like to wear a clerical collar. He said that they didn't fit. The small gold cross pin seemed to be enough to prove that he was a spiritual advisor, which was the criteria for admittance to the private area unless you were a close family member.

A familiar buzzer sounded. Steev pushed open the doors, his best black and white Nike tennis shoes making a tacky sound against the linoleum floor.

They heard him speak: "I am here for Amanda Fleming."

Winston walked over to Fran and Mildred. "You didn't eat any breakfast," Winston reminded Fran, but his glance had a question in it for Mildred.

"I am not hungry, but I am thirsty," Fran admitted. She had not eaten that morning, but that was a common strategy. She had not been told to fast for the procedure. She hadn't eaten breakfast because eating in the morning could trigger inconvenient digestive issues later that could impede the successful completion of a biopsy.

Winston nodded, but he didn't offer to do anything about it. "I will be over there and let you girls catch up," he said, withdrawing. He walked right past the water cooler and the stack of white cone-shaped cups.

"He will see the water cooler in a little while," Fran predicted. "Men don't see everything in the room. You can't blame them for that. They just don't see everything."

A tall lanky man, Winston lowered himself into a chair against the panel of windows. Then, he reached into his side pocket for a cell phone though he didn't get many calls, few texts, and didn't care about sports.

Fran grinned. "Winston reads books on his telephone. Books on a telephone! It just doesn't make any sense. But you can install a Kindle app on your telephone and read a book downloaded from Amazon on it. Books on a telephone. It doesn't make any sense to me at all."

"Why aren't you downstairs getting that biopsy?" Mildred asked.

"This is the emergency. My procedure isn't. I was there when they called a social worker for Janie," Fran explained. "I didn't want you to face a social worker by yourself. I hear she has some papers she needs to get Janie to sign. Who is this woman? Do we know who she is?"

"I think she is called Adelaide. I don't know a last name," Mildred said, rising.

Mildred walked across the room and poured two cups of water from the cooler. She took one to Winston, who nodded his thanks and then looked surprised to be holding a cup of water. He sipped it gingerly as if he was afraid that it might not be water. And then, accepting it was, he drank it all and crumpled the cup in his hand before Mildred could deliver the other cup of water to Fran.

Fran drank all of hers in little sips, tasting the coolness, breathing mindfully, being in the moment with her best friend and a baby coming and her husband across the room. *There is Winston.* Fran's eyes beheld Winston while she talked with her best friend.

Mildred went back to the cooler and refilled her friend's cup and poured herself one this time, juggling the paper cups gingerly.

Fran held her small cup thoughtfully. "You know, one way or the other, I will be all right. And you will be yourself again in a little while. You just need a little space, and some time to write your meditations. It is Janie and the baby that matter today."

"Janie told me about the social worker last night. That feels like a long time ago, but it was just yesternight. I was standing in the hallway outside her bedroom, and Janie was holding the door close like she does. She hasn't let me in that room since she got home from jail. Last night, she was fit to be tied. She told me she was giving up Little Mister and that a social worker was helping her." Mildred turned toward Fran, who pulled her feet up and sat upright again, listening.

"I couldn't process what she meant at first. And then I heard her. She was giving up the baby and going to leave my house and go somewhere. Anywhere! And that was the moment I felt relief—like a big burden was going to be taken off my shoulders. I was relieved, Frannie. I am older than I have ever been; and just between us, our girl has been hard to live with."

Fran took measured sips of her water, listening priestlike to her best friend's sobering confession. Though some congregations did not allow women to be priests, church ladies heard one another's confessions all the time and offered the priestly reassuring pardon of understanding and acceptance.

"You haven't said much about that, but I know the girl's been staying in her room. It was like she was still in jail, only in a different cell."

"Night and day. Crying. Wouldn't talk. We have been having our very limited conversations through a closed door, mostly. But that is not the point. When Janie told me her plan about giving up Little Mister, a part of me that I prefer to pretend doesn't exist, could let her go. Yesterday at Jake's party I talked with his boss about that."

"About the baby?" Fran asked, surprised.

Mildred shook her head emphatically. "No. Jake's boss Dr. Wren asked me how I could spot a ringer—something Jake said to her about me. And so, I pointed four people out to her that I thought were ringers. And when I did, she was standing next to the worst ringer in the room."

Mildred felt herself go cold, cringing at how temptation had risen up in small talk, and she had succumbed to showing off, pointing out ringers—innocent people at a party who were guests, not ringers. Not really.

"Why would Jake say that about you to his boss? That ringer thing?"

"I don't know. But it felt like praise, and I fell for it. I told Dr. Wren that spotting a ringer means you see how someone is pretending to be someone he or she is not, and when you see that you have to believe it because there are so many voices in your head accusing you of bias or some other wrongheaded concept."

"There is some truth to that," Fran allowed.

"And then I was a ringer again after I got home. Janie told me she was giving up the baby, and though I said all the right words to ask her not to do that, in my heart for an instant, I let her go. Little Mister, too. In my very heart, I let them both go. You can dress yourself up in all kinds of outfits that suggest you are someone to be admired--a church lady, a retired school teacher with a good reputation, or even some kind of a good Samaritan. The truth is I felt relief that someone I had agreed to take care of and her baby, too, were leaving.

"I know that about myself. I am a ringer even now after all these years. I know that again because I have seen it before in me. I know it. And now you know it, too."

Mildred turned in her chair, both feet planted on the floor, the paper cup unthinkingly wadded up in one palm. She had not meant to do that. Mildred always reused the flimsy paper cups if she wanted a refill. Too late now.

"Since Janie has come home, the girl has mainly been in that one room. Even so, locked up like that, the girl has been taking up a lot of space. A lot of space," Mildred repeated, as she fooled with the ball of paper in her hands. It wasn't an excuse for being a ringer; it was an explanation.

Winston looked up; his gaze curious but not intrusive. Fran nodded in his direction, *I see you, my sweetheart. I'm all right over here. So is Mildred. We are just talking. Nothing bad is going to happen here today.*

Fran lowered her voice, settling back in the chair. She wanted another cup of water but was waiting. "Many people are like that. Usually, it is a man who takes up a lot of space, but some women do, too. Liz does," Fran said, but there was no judgment in that statement. She was just taking a kind of inventory.

Mildred nodded unnecessarily. She and Fran knew one another.

"That man over there. That Winston. My guy takes up just the right amount of space," Fran said approvingly.

Winston was concentrating on his phone, squinting occasionally, and shifting the angle of the screen to find lighting that made it easier to see.

"Do you know what he is reading?" Fran asked, a smile playing at the corners of her mouth.

Mildred didn't answer. It was a rhetorical question.

"He is reading a James Michener novel about Texas. He has been reading it for weeks. He is a slow reader, but he keeps at it. Sometimes, his lips move while he reads, and I think that is so lovable. Just adorable."

"*Texas* is a good book," Mildred said. "It took me weeks to read it, too. All of Michener's books are big or, at least, the ones I know about are."

Mildred didn't add that she usually read more than one book at a time, and rotated them, reading what she felt in the mood to enjoy. Whenever she had felt trapped—which wasn't very often—Mildred had read on *Texas*. It had taken her two months to finish reading it.

"I almost want to read it just because Winston has enjoyed it so much. But I won't," Fran declared easily, stretching out her legs again. She wanted to stand up and pace the floor. "I don't like to be still as long as Winston does. Truthfully, Mildred, Winston is more of a reader than I am. He is more like you that way."

Fran hesitated and then asked the question. "Is it a done deal with this social worker? Has Janie signed the last document?"

"I don't know. When Janie told me about the social worker, it sounded like a done deal."

Fran watched Winston swipe the screen on his cell phone. "We all have second thoughts," she said, cryptically.

"We are all only human and at different times in our lives, we are truly confused. Or conflicted. Or just worn out. Mostly, that is the truth of what you felt yesterday when she told you about giving up the baby. Yesterday was a long day. A very long day. You were tired, Mildred. A lot of people who make sorrowful decisions are just tired. The girl is tired. I saw it in her. Janie is really tired. Tired of being alone. Tired of being afraid.

"Steev is in the back with Janie now. Maybe he can talk some sense into her. The boy is younger than we are. And he doesn't have to live with her so he isn't conflicted. You have heard him preach. He can be convincing," Fran said.

"No matter how tired we were yesterday, we are not giving up on Janie and Little Mister today," Mildred vowed.

"See? You are that person too," Fran said. She was still thirsty and would get another cup of water in a minute. She knew how to be thirsty; she knew how to wait. "Downstairs, the lady at the front desk was nice about me changing my mind about the biopsy today—like she thought I was scared or something and that I was just making up an excuse to get out of having a long needle stuck into my not very big breast."

Fran looked down at her breast with a kind of idle curiosity, as if she had forgotten it until just recently. And she had. She inhaled deeply and positioned herself to stand up. "But I am not scared, Mildred. I know people expect me to be; but I am not, and I don't want to have to act scared just to make other people feel useful in trying to reassure me, make me comfortable. I am not afraid," Fran explained, shrugging lightly. "I am inconvenienced. I have lived long enough to know what fear is, and I can put fear and cancer in its place when there is work to be done."

"Is that what we're doing?" Mildred asked.

It was awfully early in the morning to be working.

"That is what we are doing," Fran declared emphatically. "Waiting is a kind of work. We are working. We are going to make sure this girl knows her own mind before she makes a decision that could be worse than the one that caused her to get involved with that man who ran out on her and left her like this."

Mildred nodded that she had heard Fran.

Winston looked up and smiled again. "We are at the Alamo. It is not looking good."

Leaning closer to Mildred, her gaze still on her husband, Fran said, "We will get Janie squared away, and then we will just take one day at a time with this setback I am having." Fran held up her right hand and three fingers.

And that is when Mildred saw her best friend look hard at trouble and make her plan. It was different than looking for an escape from trouble. Fran looked at trouble head-on, eyes wide open fearlessly.

"If it is cancer you talk to three doctors: the surgeon, the radiologist, and the oncologist. After whatever needs to happen happens, they monitor you every three months for a while. Everybody who does anything to you monitors you. Then you start taking a pill if you need to reduce your estrogen, and people act like that is no big deal, but there are side effects. When all is said and done, you know I am not afraid and so I don't need reassurance, but I am going to need lots of pampering." Fran smiled convincingly as she stamped one foot emphatically on the hospital's linoleum floor. "Don't think I won't be milking this setback for all it is worth. I am going to need a lot of pampering. Winston doesn't know that yet, but you do."

"I do know. Go for it." Mildred encouraged.

This was Fran. Looking ahead. Sounding like herself. Saying she wanted pampering, and Mildred knowing that Fran didn't need pampering any more than she needed reassurances to alleviate a fear she didn't have.

Fran was saying those words so that her friends would have something to do that felt like helping, and in that way Fran was helping her friends to be consoled and unafraid.

That was Fran. Mildred knew it all and played her part, giving the help Fran needed by accepting the challenge to be helpful, and all the while they were getting through it—every moment that was involved would be consecrated to the nature of Love that was expressed and lived out just like this.

"What do you want? Here I am. I can come or I can go—whatever you need. I can take up space or leave it to you. Your choice," Mildred said.

"I am glad you asked, because once this thing gets into full swing, and I don't mean this biopsy. If harder stuff happens, you know the Bereans are going to want to help us newlyweds. And you know the girls. I am sure the other Bereans will need some guidance about what will help Winston and me the most." Fran cut her blue eyes at Mildred, and they were merry with amusement.

She hadn't eaten breakfast, had canceled a necessary medical procedure, was facing the possibility of cancer, and she was playful in a waiting room that was too cold.

"To the best of your ability will you try to keep Belle Deerborn from bringing over that tuna fish casserole she makes."

Mildred stifled a grimace and nodded. "Belle does love to make that tuna fish casserole. I think it is because she usually has all of the ingredients for it in the house in the pantry and the fridge. Sam is the one to blame for this tuna casserole being Belle's signature dish that she takes to people recovering from setbacks. He never told her that they are too soupy, too cheesy, and too fishy. He just kept eating them."

"Men," Fran said, still watching Winston. "On a different note, tuna fish casserole aside, this is a rare opportunity for me to rack up on everything I want, like small cans of coffee. Opening a can of coffee can start your day just right, so I don't want any more big cans of coffee coming to the house. It takes too long to drink them. Small cans empty out in a few days, and we get to open another one. Aroma therapy! And butter! Half sticks of Land 'O Lakes butter. Speaking of butter, use it in your Christmas fudge. Winston has never had your Christmas fudge. I want him to have it," Fran said, fiercely.

"Anytime you feel like Christmas," Mildred promised.

"I will want that fudge sooner rather than later, and I want the fudge to be still warm." Look ahead, Fran smiled more to herself than to Mildred. "Oh, how I want to see Winston take that first bite of your warm Christmas fudge. I want to be looking right at my darling when his eyes come up from the container of fudge you bring over, and which Anne Henry has wrongly said is too big. She said people don't need that much fudge. But they do. At certain points in their lives, people need as much fudge as they can get."

"Anne Henry doesn't understand fudge," Mildred murmured, for the words still stung that Anne Henry had said that about her fudge. 'It's too much. I only need two pieces.'

"But I want Winston to know Christmas—our kind of Christmas--through your fudge. I want to share it with him."

"Just tell me when," Mildred repeated.

"And this is a tricky bit, and I can't see how it can be done. We will have to pray over it. We are going to get rid of those scented trash bags we use at Winston's house. On my best day the smell of that scented trash bag makes me nauseas."

"Throw them away now," Mildred advised immediately.

"Oh, honey. You are such an infant. Right now, I can't do that. You see that old man over there? Previously my fiancé and now my new bridegroom."

Mildred studied Winston, who was reading about the Alamo and shaking his head sadly.

"He bought those scented trash bags especially for me. It was his idea of a wedding gift. My honey bought his new bride a big monster box of scented trash bags and had them waiting for me on the kitchen counter at his house because once—just once—when we walked into his closed-up house it smelled stale, and I said something like that. I think I said, 'we need to open a window" and he heard me. The trash in the kitchen had not been emptied in a couple of days, and he blamed my displeasure on that so he decided to fix it. My sweet old boy gave me scented trash bags as a homecoming present, a welcome home present, too, as in, mi casa is your casa now. He was as proud of his idea as if the scent of those trash bags was the same fragrance as Chanel No. 5."

"You stopped wearing perfume when Gritz died," Mildred recalled, the memory coming to the surface just like that.

Fran nodded. "It was too much. I stopped wearing Chanel No. 5 after Gritz, and I don't regret it. It was survival really. And so is this next move. We have got to get rid of those scented trash bags and in such a way that Winston doesn't go and buy another box when we run out of these. I just haven't figured out how. The scent of the trash bags has somehow become the signature aroma of my current love affair with that old man over there. He is fighting with his heroes at the Alamo right now. Look at him. I love him to bits, and I hate those scented trash bags."

As if knowing she were talking about him, Winston looked up at smiled. A question formed in his eyes, but his gaze drifted to Mildred, and he smiled, giving them space.

"What else do you want?" Mildred repeated the question. She was relaxing, the tension in her shoulders easing. Belle had Chase. Sam, too. Steev was talking sense to Janie, wasn't he? And she had all that she needed to make Christmas fudge anytime Fran wanted it.

"Winston would enjoy a roast beef dinner one night when we are recovering. A roast beef dinner with potatoes and carrots and Vidalia onions because my guy over there is a meat eater."

"Do you want the Christmas fudge the same night?"

Fran considered the idea. "No. I want that peach cobbler your mother used to make. Winston would like that peach cobbler. I want the Christmas fudge to come on a crisp cool afternoon about four o'clock when I am almost myself again. I want it to snow that afternoon, Mildred. I want a sweet dusting of snow at twilight just as you arrive with the warm fudge. Can you arrange that?" she asked.

"Consider it done," Mildred promised easily.

"And while it is snowing, I want a family of deer to pass slowly by my front window. Winston and I will eat your Christmas fudge together, watching the deer linger in the snow in the front yard."

"Okay," Mildred agreed, just as the door opened and a woman in an old-fashioned dollar-green bank teller suit came in holding a brown leather briefcase in one hand and a taupe vinyl shoulder bag drooping off the other shoulder.

Both women stopped talking then. The woman in the doorway was a stranger to Mildred and Fran. But they knew who she was. This was the social worker who was coming to get Janie to sign some kind of paper and take Little Mister away.

That made her the enemy.

HELPING THE SOCIAL WORKER

"Are you looking for someone?" Winston asked, rising. A deacon in the church--but never an elder because he didn't want to be--Winston stretched out his hand, automatically extending the right hand of fellowship.

The woman was startled but responded, walking purposefully toward him, shifting her purse and her briefcase to free one hand. "I am Janie's friend Adelaide," she said, gripping Winston's hand forcefully. She looked around the room, incongruously searching for the young pregnant woman she had come to find.

"Who does she think she is going to find here? Why would a pregnant woman be sitting in the waiting room?" Fran hissed under her breath.

Then rising, to go stand beside Winston, Fran turned and winked at Mildred and said, "Ding dong. We may have ourselves a ringer. This might turn out to be easier than we thought."

"Girls, this kind lady is Miss Adelaide," Winston called out. "And she is looking for little Janie to help her with some government paperwork. I told her that you were looking after little Janie and would help her."

"Not the government exactly," Adelaide interjected carefully, her eyes canny with watchfulness. Her smile was polite but not hospitable.

Fran smiled first, patting Adelaide's forearm, as she beamed her greeting, "How kind you are to come so quickly and so early. You can't predict when a baby will come. But it is always a great day when they do!" Fran said, clapping her hands together the way Gritz had when he was gleeful.

"It is my job to be here," Adelaide replied stiffly, her voice gravelly and too loud for the room. "Somebody downstairs called me to come. Janie asked for me," she added.

The woman's A-line polyester skirt was wrinkled and slightly twisted.

Both Mildred and Fran wanted to reach over and adjust the skirt so that the button and zipper were better lined up in the back. Their friends did that for one another all the time in the ladies' room at church. *Honey, you're all twisted.*

Fran nodded, stepped closer to Adelaide, and whispered confidentially, "Janie is in the back with the medical folks. They are measuring things. You know how that works," she suggested, nodding gently to prompt the other woman to agree.

Adelaide wriggled her nose, repulsed by the idea of medical measuring, dismissing the explanation with a wave of her bejeweled hand. She wore lots of shiny rings, but none of them were real diamonds. "I just need a quick signature. Won't take half a minute," she declared. "If she had just let me come over yesterday when we spoke it would all be done right now."

Adelaide turned toward the locked double doors that led to the back where the laboring mothers-to-be were monitored.

Mildred spoke without planning to, the news coming out of nowhere. "The preacher is with Janie right now. Our preacher," she amended. "From the church on the corner."

"Paster Steev is new on the job, and you know how a new preacher wants to prove himself and what he has learned so recently in seminary," Fran said. "He is very young and very enthusiastic. You know how enthusiastic a young preacher can be and how long they can talk."

Adelaide blinked rapidly, digesting the implications of this news. She looked behind her at the door and then around the room for some other means of escape.

"Pastor Steev is praying with Janie--for her and the baby," Fran explained, shaking her head ruefully. "And she is in labor. Can you imagine?"

"Painful," Adelaide opined. "Poor girl. Do we need to rescue her? I can go back there. When it is necessary, I can use my sharp elbows to get to where I need to be." Adelaide made a move towards the locked doors that led to the back where mothers-to-be in labor endured.

"I shouldn't disturb a pastor though, should I?" Adelaide asked, stopping herself. Her cell phone buzzed in her shoulder bag, and she looked down at it, curious but not reaching for it.

"Oh, no. We can't disturb a preacher while he is praying," Fran said quickly. "Just between us and St. Pete's gatepost, our sweet young preacher is kind of long-winded," Fran added. "We didn't expect that in such a young man. Long-winded, is what I mean. Older men are usually long-winded. Younger men, not so much. But Brother Steev is. Little Janie is unchurched presently, and you know how long a preacher will pray when he thinks the person beside him doesn't go to church?"

Adelaide nodded with resignation. "Preachers do like to talk." She eyed the clock. It was almost 10:30. The second hand moved and then moved again. Time passed slowly for women in labor and for those waiting for them in the waiting room.

"Do you have a home church?" Fran asked, brightly. "We go to the church on the corner. That is not its official name, but that is what we all call it."

The other woman's eyes grew veiled with the mystery of whether she belonged to a church or not.

"Because if you are not churched, when the preacher comes out he is going to come right over here, and he will start talking to you. That is going to be one of the first things he will ask you. In no time at all, Pastor Steev will know if you need prayer. You will be taken to the chapel downstairs, and he won't let you leave until you are prayed up. That is what he calls it. Praying you up. Brother Steev is a good preacher who takes his job seriously."

Leaning closer, Fran confided to the social worker, "Hell is very real to our young preacher, and you know how a preacher can pray when hell is very real to him, and he suspects that someone standing in front of him might be headed there."

Adelaide's eyes widened. She drew back her shoulders, and Mildred saw that the old-fashioned shoulder pads in her green blazer were not lined up evenly. The left shoulder pad had slipped, giving her a tilted quality.

Adelaide took a long slow breath and nodded, swapping a meaningful glance with Fran. "I have seen a lot of hell in my work. I don't need to hear about anymore of it." She eyed the swinging doors with concern and looked around the room. *Where would be the best place to be if the preacher came out and how could she stay out of his way until he was gone?*

Fran looked contemplative. "It might be a good idea if we all took a little break from this very cold room until Pastor Steev is prayed up with Janie, and then we girls can do what needs to be done," Fran suggested. "My husband over there—the man who welcomed you—will keep an eye out for us, and text us when it is safe to come back. Won't you, Winston?" Fran called over to him.

His gaze shot up. "You know I will," he said, and went back to Texas.

In that moment, Adelaide assumed that Mildred and Fran were her allies against a preacher who prayed for others who didn't believe hell was real.

HELLO HARLO

Fran patted Adelaide's arm again, getting her attention. "Have you even had a cup of coffee yet, honey?"

"Just barely. It is out in the car." Adelaide shook her head. "I had to park in the deck. I don't like parking decks."

"Oh, my dear. Parking decks are not our friend. I can never remember which level I am on."

"I took a picture of my level and my car," Adelaide admitted. "It's 4." She nodded, confirming her memory. "I'm on Level 4."

"There was talk for a while that a woman was kidnapped from the parking Level 4, but she wasn't, so you must relax if that is what you are worrying about. Turns out after they found her body that they learned she made it out of the parking lot here at the hospital but got kidnapped over at the Piggly Wiggly. If you think a parking deck is dangerous, you need to think about the transient traffic in a grocery store parking lot," Fran warned. "Speaking of Piggly Wiggly and food, I think we all need a little something to hold body and soul together."

Fran waved a hand at Winston, who looked up. "The girls and I will be back in a little while. Do you need anything?"

Grieving the situation at the Alamo, Winston cast a baleful glance at Adelaide and Mildred and told Fran, "Nope."

"Will you hold down the fort, Winston?" Fran asked the same question a different way.

This time, he gave her a thumbs-up and a quick nod. "I am not going anywhere," he promised.

Fran raised two fingers in a Boy Scout salute, but did not touch the brow of her head. Instead, she pressed the two fingers to her mouth, kissed them, waved the kiss good-bye to Winston, and led the way out of the room to the elevator.

"I am so ready to get out of there," Fran confided to Adelaide, taking her arm companionably. "I don't like waiting rooms or hospitals for that matter. It is kind of an in-between time. A little late for breakfast. A little early for lunch. But Adelaide, Millie and I—she's my friend here— are going to take you down this hallway to the hospital coffee shop where we can all eat a little something to keep body and soul together. We can enjoy a light repast and give the preacher time to leave. Then, we will come back here and do what needs to be done."

"I really should stay here, I suppose," Adelaide objected half-heartedly. "I have got some papers the Baby Mama needs to sign." Adelaide was repeating herself.

Everyone did sooner or later.

"Nobody is going back there to be with Janie until the preacher comes out," Fran asserted. "Do you eat bacon?" she asked suddenly. "Because the coffee shop here has really good bacon. You remember the bacon I am talking about, Millie?"

"Oh, yes," Mildred said. "It is Zeigler's black pepper bacon. That is all they use here."

"It is very good," Fran confirmed, as the overhead hallway light flickered.

Adelaide looked up, distracted. The fluorescent light was unkind to Adelaide. Her face was pale with strain, and the etchings of time about her mouth and eyes were revealed starkly.

"It does that," Fran explained. "Nothing to worry about."

Fran did not know if the flickering light was nothing to worry about. Had she been home, Fran would have fretted about the flickering light and wondered what kind of bulb she needed to change it. Fran had many opinions about the merits and defects of different types of light bulbs and the wattage required in various rooms and situations. But in that moment, there was nothing to worry about except steering the social worker and the official papers needing to be signed away from Janie toward any other place.

"Once upon a time I had a bacon and tomato sandwich in the hospital coffee shop, and it was excellent. Doesn't that sound good? Bacon and tomato? And a hot cup of their good coffee not made in one of these industrial size pots they have located in the hallways, which they don't wash often enough. I was raised to wash a coffee pot every night, and a clean pot does make a difference in how good the morning coffee is. Yes, it does. At the coffee stations in this hospital, you never know how fresh the coffee is," Fran said.

The sound of Adelaide's two-inch heels clicked on the linoleum flooring. The coffee in the cup in her car was cold by now, and it was a long way back to parking Level 4. Adelaide was ready to sit down and eat a little something.

"How did you become a social worker, Addie?" Fran asked, steering them around a corner and down another hallway toward the coffee shop where her friend Harlo would be serving Zeigler's bacon sandwiches.

"I was on a jury once, and I kept voting innocent because I thought the person was innocent. Nobody else did. Eleven other people kept voting guilty. Finally, after we had to adjourn for the day and come back the next morning, a very nasty man asked me, 'Are you some kind of social worker?' and that is when I had my ah-ha moment. I thought, 'Maybe I am. Maybe I am some kind of social worker,'" Adelaide said with a mysterious smile. "Your husband will text us when the preacher leaves?"

"Of course. My husband is very dependable."

Adelaide made another confession then. She said, "I am a little hungry."

22

BRUNCHTIME

"Oh my word! What a story about being on a jury. That is amazing!" Fran said, pushing open the door to the coffee shop.

"Jury duty is a kind of wake-up call for us all, isn't it?" Fran asked, not waiting for agreement. "We are going to sit over there and let ourselves rest and eat and feel so much better. It is going to be a long day. First-time babies take a long time to come. There is Harlo. Oh, good."

Addie settled back into the chair, the cell phone in her purse buzzing intermittently. She wondered why a hospital didn't block cell phones. There was some kind of sign in the lobby that boasted it did. But her cell phone had rung three times since she had come in the building. The two ladies were so right. She was hungry. She ignored the ringing cell phone.

"You girls want to try one of these while you are figuring out what you want to eat?" Harlo, the waitress asked, as she settled a small white saucer down on the table between them. It held three itsy-bitsy muffins. The muffins were steaming, smelling of warm apple and cinnamon and dusted in brown sugar crystals.

Before they could agree, Harlo asked another question, looking past them to the door.

"Do you girls need a minute, or do you know what you want?" she asked pointedly.

Fran spoke up quickly. "Our friend here has important work to do, and she is in a hurry so we don't have much time. We have just enough time for a quick bite. But Miss Harlo, we need sweet tea and a quick bite. Could we start with some sweet iced tea all around and a small bowl of lemon slices? How long has it been since you took the time to squeeze some lemon into a glass of sweet tea, Addie?"

Before Adelaide could answer, Fran mused, "I bet you don't even let yourself drink sweet tea. You are so thin and pretty. So many people are afraid of sugar these days, but sweet tea—" Fran said. She shook her head knowledgeably. "You can walk a long ways on a glass of sweet tea. Honey, if you have got a big day ahead of you, you need to catch your breath, sip a little sweet ice tea with lemon, and take some nourishment. Life is short."

"Eat more bacon," Mildred urged, stifling a small giggle that did not come out of her very often. Neither she nor Fran had heard that giggle from Mildred in over two years; and in that moment, though the giggle was familiar, neither one could remember what had caused Mildred to giggle long ago.

Fran and Mildred stared at one another quizzically.

Who are you?

And who are you?

"Dear Addie, you are so young with your whole life ahead of you, and you think life is meant to be lived best and most efficiently in a hurry. You get a little older, and you learn soon enough that you have got to pace yourself for the long haul, Addie. Life is about living the long haul. Is that what people call you? Addie?" Fran said.

"Sometimes," the social worker said. She studied the muffins then. "The sign on the wall said this was a cafeteria, but I don't see a buffet. Why do they call it a cafeteria?"

"It is a coffee shop, but they just never changed out the sign on the wall. No one worries about that here," Fran said. "They both start with a **C** and they are both just words."

Fran pushed the small plate of muffins toward Adelaide. "Oswald is always trying to invent a new kind of muffin. And he makes jellies on top of the stove, which he wants people to put on his muffins instead of butter, though why he should care, I don't know."

"Oswald?" Adelaide repeated, her brow furrowing as she took a muffin between her thumb and her forefinger. She studied it, asking at the same time, "How do you know the muffin man's name is Oswald and that lady's name is Harlo?

"How do I know your name is Adelaide? I have visited friends in the hospital before. We come here. Don't we Mildred?"

Mildred nodded, reaching for a muffin. "Whatever fruit Oswald has got on hand, he just stirs it up with some sugar and lemon peel on the top of the stove in a sauce pan. We love Oswald. Though he doesn't come out here very often," Mildred said, using a butter knife to add a thin layer of tremulous translucent jelly pooling in a very small white bowl. It was almost a red hue, but not quite. The color of the jelly was a delicate shade. You could see through it.

Fran took a nibbling bite and nodded approvingly.

"You would think Ossie would get tired of trying new things, but he doesn't seem to. There was a kind of a jelly on what he called a peanut butter muffin the last time I was here that was interesting. Yes, that is what I would call that muffin. Interesting. But when I asked about it, Harlo, Ossie's wife--she is the one taking care of us--said that he got mixed up. Harlo said that Ossie had never planned to use peanut butter. I don't know how you would mix up peanut butter with anything else."

"He was planning to use almond butter," Mildred remembered. She smiled at Adelaide. "Nuts give you energy, so I think he was trying to produce an energy muffin."

Fran waved away the information, tilting her head. "That makes more sense. Almond butter would be lighter than peanut butter, I suspect. The muffin came out all right in spite of what he was doing. You would naturally think that peanut butter would be too heavy for the batter, but the chopped figs made it work," Fran said with a shrug. "Between us, it wasn't his best work, but it was an edible muffin. I would call it that."

"I remember that interesting muffin," Mildred recalled, looking up as Harlo returned with three glasses of sweet iced tea and a bowl of lemon slices.

"Aroma therapy," Fran breathed, looking at the bright lemon slices.

"Y'all want the special?" Harlo asked suddenly. "That's the quickest thing we make if a quick bite is really what you want."

Addie reached out for the single sheet laminated menu.

Fran automatically pressed Addie's hand down.

"Don't touch that menu, honey. Remember, you are in a hospital. How many germs do you think could be on that menu? Not everyone washes their hands like they should."

Distracted, Adelaide reached out for the glass of water, sloshing some over the side.

Fran busily mopped up the excess with her white paper napkin.

"How about three specials?" Harlo suggested. "Everybody who comes here this time of day is coming for the special. We serve 'em all day long. A bacon and tomato sandwich will keep you till dinner. We will be serving chicken noodle soup for supper, if y'all are still here."

Addie looked around the room and a half dozen people were holding bacon and tomato sandwiches and eating with appetite.

"Is it really that good?" Adelaide asked, fighting the urge to reach for the menu anyway.

"There is a reason we call it the special," Harlo replied.

Mildred giggled, and tried to hide the sound in her glass of ice tea. She took a big sip, peering over the edge of her glass.

"Oswald has a special bacon he uses," Harlo explained.

"We told her about the black pepper Zeigler's," Fran confessed with a smile.

"Some folks eating in here this time of day don't even have anyone to visit in the hospital. They just come by to have the special. The people around here have fond memories of bacon and tomato sandwiches. Oswald and I pride ourselves on that."

Addie relaxed then. "Where do you get the tomatoes?"

"We grow 'em. Oswald and I have a patch of land. People call them organic. We just call them our tomatoes. Are y'all just here for lunch, or have you got somebody to worry about?"

"Janie is in labor," Mildred said. "It is her first."

Harlo did not know who Janie was, but that didn't matter. Harlo nodded as if she understood—a move she made all day long with just about everybody who came in with a sad story. "It takes a long time to have a first baby— sometimes it won't come until the next day. One sandwich a piece gonna be enough?"

Fran nodded for them all. "May we have some more muffins?" she asked, pointing toward the saucer that contained only Adelaide's mini-muffin.

"No," Harlo replied easily. "Muffins are just for fun. You have got to spread out your fun so that there is enough for everybody all day long."

"They were really good," Mildred said.

Addie finally ate hers, automatically trying to catch the crumbs that fell first to her bosom and then on to the table.

"When is Oswald going to make jelly and put it in jars so that we can buy it and take it home?" Fran asked.

"You know my sweet man doesn't want to work that hard. And I don't either. When you preserve jellies, you have to make sure the jars are cleaned a certain way and then the lids have to be tightened a certain way. It is too much work, and then someone is likely to sue you if it didn't get airtight. Naw. Ossie's jelly is just for fun, like the muffins are just for fun. I don't know why people don't want to have more fun," Harlo said, while standing bravely in a hospital meeting place where people came for the special.

"Coffee after the special?" Harlo asked. She wasn't writing anything down, just asking and smiling and keeping her eye on the people already eating and the door to see who might come in next.

"This sweet tea is fine for me," Addie replied.

"Oh, really," Fran said, looking disappointed. " I thought we might start with sweet ice tea and maybe finish with a cup of Harlo's coffee. The coffee here is very good. They use an African bean imported from a small coffee bean farm near a mission in a faraway place—so far that the missionary drives his motorcycle up a steep hill to reach it, and brings back the beans on two saddle bags draped over the back of the motorcycle. It is pretty dangerous work, but he does it for the Lord. I have heard they might be making a movie about it."

"Three coffees for dessert," Harlo confirmed, stopping the discussion. "Is this your first time to eat here?"

"Maybe," Adelaide replied, in case *yes* was the wrong answer.

Harlo smiled. "The bacon is crispy today. Is that going to be a problem?"

"Not for me," Fran replied, sitting back in the chair.

"I like crispy bacon," Mildred confirmed.

"Whatever," Addie said, because an answer was expected of her.

"Every cup of coffee made from the special coffee beans someone drinks helps vaccinate a small child in Africa against all kinds of diseases," Fran explained. "Everybody who comes here for the special automatically drinks a cup of coffee for Jesus and his children everywhere."

"I will have some coffee then," Addie relented, looking at her wristwatch. She reached for the briefcase positioned on the floor beside her feet and patted it. The papers to be signed were safe. The cell phone in her purse buzzed again.

"Do you need to answer that?" Fran asked solicitously.

Mildred had gone quiet, breathing long and slow, long and slow. There is a kind of praying you can do while other people are talking about coffee beans, and Mildred was doing that kind of praying. She was in labor with Janie, and it was that kind of prayer, a laboring prayer.

"Coming up," Harlo said, as Fran eyed the clock on the wall.

"And could you make an extra sandwich to go?" Fran asked. "Winston's upstairs."

"Oh, sweet Winston. I am so glad he is still alive," Harlo said, turning toward the kitchen and Oswald who kept the crispy bacon and the sliced tomatoes and the homemade mayonnaise he used on his toasted sandwiches. They hadn't talked about Ossie's homemade mayonnaise, but it was his secret ingredient for every popular sandwich in the shop. The key? His mayonnaise, like his mini muffins, was made fresh daily.

"Will this take long? There is a couple who wants that baby, and I kind of promised them that I would not fail to deliver. People know me. I have a reputation to maintain, and I always deliver."

"Oh, honey. That is so sweet," Fran said, reaching over and patting the hand that reached for the briefcase. "Nobody fails when they are doing God's work."

The glint of Fran's engagement ring caught Addie's eye. Her own bejeweled fingers didn't shine quite as truly.

Fran wiggled her left hand playfully. "I am just back from my honeymoon," Fran boasted. "I like how big the diamond is. I know you are not supposed to show off, but it is a very pretty ring and that man you met who is holding down the fort gave it to me. That is my Winston. He will text me if someone comes out about Janie, so you don't need to worry. He can read a book on his telephone, and he knows how to text."

The sandwiches arrived on hand-cut slices of toasted honey wheat bread. Slices of fragrant juicy tomatoes peeked out of two sides. Thick pieces of pepper bacon were also coated in homemade mayonnaise.

The first bite was perfect.

So was the second bite.

Adelaide began to moan slightly as she ate, blotting her lips that were smeared with oozing homemade mayonnaise. "I was starving."

"Of course you were, honey. You work too hard. You better take care of your health now because later is too late."

Adelaide began to relax then. Her cell phone buzzed two more times. She ignored it, chewing with her eyes partially closed, shutting out the world, and her head drifting slightly backwards, looking at the world for a moment in time with heavy-lidded lizard eyes.

When they were halfway finished with the sandwiches, Harlo brought three cups of steaming coffee.

The three women each took a first sip, blinking and registering the taste. It was very strong. Addie put the cup down on the table with resolve.

Fran emptied three capsules of Half & Half into her cup.

Mildred settled back in her chair and never let go of her cup. She loved it.

Adelaide took cautious sips of the strong coffee but went back and forth, sipping sweet tea, then coffee.

Harlo watched and winked at Mildred. With one wave of one finger Harlo pointed to bags of coffee anyone could take for a donation to the Cause. There was a can with a slot in the top beside it and pictures of a child at a clinic on the front of the can getting a life-saving shot of a vaccine.

Finally, Harlo did bring more muffins but only in one small folded waxy paper sack and these she handed to Adelaide. "First time diners get more so's you can have an afternoon snack later," Harlo explained with a conspiratorial wink.

And then shrugging, she said, "Sorry, girls. You are repeat offenders. Old-timers. No more muffins for you today."

"But here is sweet Winston's sandwich, and maybe there is a muffin in there. Maybe two," Harlo said with another wink.

Harlo hid a smile as she placed a check face down on the table top. Adelaide stared at it as if she didn't know what it was.

"Oh, let me, Addie." Fran offered. "This is on my husband. I am still on my honeymoon, and the man who gave me this diamond ring loves to make me happy."

While Adelaide was absorbing that idea, Mildred walked over to the counter by the register and inserted a folded twenty-dollar bill in Harlo's collection box, took one bag of coffee and walked it back to the social worker, and said, "Honey, this is for you. We are so proud of the good work you are doing for mamas and babies. Remember, when you drink this tomorrow and the next day you will be helping vaccinate other babies all across the world."

They hugged, offering small air kisses that sometimes happened among church ladies, whatever the denomination. In the South, people did kissing.

They visited the ladies' room, stopped at the hospital gift shop where Mrs. Simmons stocked hand-crocheted baby booties made by a circle over at the Methodist church and who donated them to the hospital gift shop. No one knew how the profits from the sale of the booties were spent, and no one worried about it. For in the South there are volunteer church ladies working everywhere they are needed in coffee shops and gift shops and Emporiums and grocery stores, and they know each other instantly and in the knowing don't ask questions that have only one answer. *We are here for Love's sake. Oh, yes.*

Adelaide stood back while Fran and Mildred each bought a pair of booties, one blue and the other yellow. Then, smiling to themselves, they steered Adelaide back to the waiting room, where they found Winston just where they had left him.

Fran handed him the sack with the sandwich and said, "Harlo sends her warm regards. She is glad you are alive."

"I am glad I am alive, too," Winston replied, opening the sack. He sat down and peeled back the wax paper, looked up and grinned. "That Harlo!"

"It's black pepper bacon," Adelaide offered. "And Oswald makes his own mayonnaise." She eyed Winston's sandwich with interest.

He grinned and said before taking his first bite. "The preacher is still in the back. Nurse came out and said things are slowing down. Gonna be a long, long day."

"That preacher really is long winded," Adelaide agreed, eyeing the closed doors and the clock on the wall. "I have been here ninety minutes, and I have another appointment. I will have to come back later today."

"Oh, yes. Later today...." Fran urged. "You have got so much on your plate, and you were so precious to spend some of your time with us. So precious. Isn't she precious?" Fran asked Mildred, who nodded.

"Does she serve those bacon and tomato sandwiches for supper too?" Adelaide asked suddenly.

"Until they run out of tomatoes. Then they offer chicken soup. That doesn't sound so very glamourous, but just between us, there have been people dying in beds in this hospital who were given a bowl of Oswald's chicken noodle soup instead of what they were offered from the hospital kitchen, and that chicken soup raised them from the dead. It will give you a boost. That's for sure. I may want a bowl of that soup later if we are still here for suppertime."

"That sounds good," Mildred said. "Winston, do you think you would like a bowl of Oswald's chicken noodle soup later?"

"Girls, if you want soup, I want soup," Winston said agreeably. He was enjoying his sandwich, saving the two apple cinnamon muffins for dessert.

"We will see," Fran predicted, not sitting down. Adelaide didn't either.

Now it was just a question of getting her out the door.

Adelaide pulled out a business card and tried to figure out which lady to leave it with. She studied Mildred, remembered something Janie had said, and then turned to Fran and asked, "Will you call me when it is time to come back?"

"I surely will," Fran promised sweetly. "When it is time to come back."

And as Adelaide nodded and walked away Fran muttered darkly, "I will call you when we give Little Mister his first birthday party. That will be about the right time."

23

JANIE'S FAMILY

Adelaide had not been gone thirty minutes when the double doors to the area where laboring mothers-to-be were tended opened. A nurse with a clipboard called out, "Family of Amanda Fleming. Goes by Janie."

"I had forgotten that was her last name," Fran said, rising before Mildred could digest what she had just heard.

"I am Mrs. Holmes. You want us," Fran declared, still enjoying the newness of her last name and her status as Winston's wife.

"Which one of you is the mother or the grandmother?" the nurse asked perfunctorily.

Her manner irked Fran. "We take turns," Fran replied smoothly, her demeanor daring the other woman to object to that response. Fran smiled a dare as her chin went up. Oswald's strong coffee was very potent. One cup of it, and you could be anyone you needed to be.

Before Mildred could launch into a more precise explanation, Fran waved away the need for more words— more small talk-- and pointed to her best friend. "We are the ones who are here for Janie."

"It is slow going. It is going to be a long day," the nurse complained, leading the way. "She said something about a social worker coming to see her."

"Janie told us something, too. But there is no social worker here," Fran said, her bright blue eyes wide now—her smile trustworthy.

The nurse tapped in her security code, and the heavy doors swung open. "Watch your step. There is a sticky place there where some people stumble."

Both Mildred and Fran studied the floor, automatically falling into a single line behind their guide, matching their footsteps to where the nurse placed her feet.

"Your girl is putting on quite a show," the nurse said over her shoulder, as she led the way. There was a hitch in her stride.

Mildred breathed a joy prayer in the nurse's direction. On their way to Janie, they passed other women in beds. Husbands, boyfriends, and mothers were standing beside them. *Oh. That's why the waiting room was empty.* She saw Steev standing in a prayer circle with a large family around the bed of another moaning mother-to-be. Head bowed, he stopped to pray with them after leaving Janie. He didn't see them. Room after room, significant others were with the women about to give birth.

"We are in here," the nurse said, pointing toward a cubicle with an open door. She leaned back against the open door, waiting for them to pass through.

Janie was lying in a mound of rumpled bedclothes, wearing a thin gown that did nothing to make her feel protected or safe. When she looked up at them, her eyes were dull, dazed. Her shoulders had rounded. She was beaten by the moment and bowed down by what was ahead.

"Your girl is a screamer. Maybe you can help her with that," the nurse said.

Fran never encountered a bully that could make her back down, and she didn't in that moment either. "Fear makes pain feel worse. Often, a young person hasn't lived long enough to have learned coping skills needed for pain management."

The nurse dealt with all kinds of people all day long and didn't spend any time trying to figure out why this little woman in front of her had an attitude. The nurse ignored Fran's argument, reciting her spiel. "Mother can go home tomorrow at the latest if that baby gets a move-on. Women don't need to spend a whole night in the hospital just to have a baby. Hospitals are for sick people."

Mildred saw Fran's fist curl and stepped in front of her. "Being pregnant isn't being sick. Being in pain...." Mildred began before the nurse interrupted her.

"People don't want to take care of each other anymore. That is one of the big problems in this world. A lot of people here just don't have nobody else to take care of them."

"Our girl has everybody she needs," Mildred said, as Fran's fist unfurled.

"Once that baby gets here we can start counting down the hours till she goes home where you two can take care of her. You look like you know what to do," the nurse remarked, giving Mildred the once over.

People often assumed that Mildred knew more than she did. Teaching fifth graders was one kind of work, but Mildred had never taken care of a newborn baby in her entire life. And she did not know what to do for a young woman who had just given birth. *What kind of personal care would Janie need?* Surely, there would be a pamphlet or some written instructions on how to take care of a new mother and the baby. Mildred handled a challenge best if she had some written instructions to follow.

"I will check in on you gals later," the nurse said, backing out of the room. They waited for her to reach midway down the hall before they all started talking at once.

"She is the meanest woman I have ever met," Janie declared, sitting up in the bed and leaning forward, arching her chest toward the foot of the bed. It was a strange position for a woman as pregnant as she.

Janie stretched her neck and moved her head back and forth as if there was something biting into her skin. She looked miserable. "I have been in jail, and this is worse."

"It won't be for long, Janie-girl. Millie and I are here now, and we won't let anything bad happen to you," Fran vowed.

"When Steev was here, that old nurse was sweet as can be. Sweet as can be! But as soon as Steev left, she became the..." Janie raised a hand and pointed to the door way. "The woman you saw."

A sudden contraction stopped Janie from saying more. Fran held Janie's hand and murmured soothing words. Mildred shifted her position and placed her hand on Janie's foot. Bare nervous toes squirmed under the touch. Looking around Mildred wondered what had happened to the mink-trimmed slippers.

"What did Steev talk about?" Fran asked, trying to distract Janie from her pain.

"I don't know exactly," Janie admitted. "He said a lot of words, but I couldn't tell exactly what he was talking about." She sighed heavily, perspiration dripping down both sides of her face. "He wouldn't leave. And I looked like this.

When the pains came, his jaw tightened. I could tell he wanted to do something for me, but he did not know what to do. But he stayed anyway," Janie reported. Wonder filling her eyes, she said, "I wanted him to go, but he stayed, and when he stayed I was glad, but I still wanted him to go."

"We understand," Fran acknowledged throatily. "We really do."

Janie returned Fran's handclasp and nodded, leaning her head back against the sweat-soaked pillow.

Mildred walked over to the closet and opened the door. There were two more pillows in there, fresh and clean. She lifted one out and took it to Janie's bedside. Wordlessly, Mildred took the sodden pillow and replaced it with the clean, cool one.

"You are staying too," Janie remarked, with wonder. She leaned her head back with eyes closed. A tremble overtook her legs—a chill of some kind--and it passed through her like an electric current. "My body is not my own," she said to no one in particular. "Just before Steev left, he placed a hand on my head and prayed for me, but he whispered cloudlike words, and I couldn't tell what he said to God about me in front of me, but he was talking kind of behind my back, too. Private, like. But I didn't mind it too much. He wouldn't leave, until he had to leave. But I don't know why he had to leave. I told him about the social worker, and he just said that everything would be all right. It's hard to believe that, but I believed him."

Janie's legs trembled again, and both Fran and Mildred tucked the thin blanket around her legs, each one sitting on either side of the narrow hospital bed, anchoring the girl in the safety of their presence.

"You aren't going to leave either," Janie concluded finally, her focus on something distant from where they were.

"We told you we wouldn't," Mildred reminded her.

It was the first time since the girl had come home when she heard the words and believed them.

The pains continued, but the girl was less loud about them. In time, the nurse returned to assess Janie's status and say with no feeling at all when she made the announcement, "It's time to take her to the next room. You girls can't go with her now."

Fran and Mildred ignored the nurse, walking alongside the bed as the nurse with the bum knee pushed it down the hallway.

Both women waved as Janie was rolled through another pair of swinging doors. Fran called out, "We will be here waiting for you."

Mildred wanted to speak; but she felt weak, and her mouth was too dry to talk.

Fran shot her a glance. "You better go on back to Janie's room and stay out of that nurse's way. She is looking for a fight, and we don't want one."

"You were the one who wanted to punch her," Mildred said.

"I did. But I am over it now," Fran admitted. "Who knows what goes on in the mind of someone like her?"

"Maybe her shift will finish soon, and we will get a nicer nurse in a better mood."

"She is not going anywhere anytime soon," Mildred predicted.

Fran nodded in agreement. "She has been here long enough to write her own ticket. Tomorrow when we get this baby and our girl home, we won't even remember her."

Mildred stared at her friend, considering what the future would bring for them both.

"I am going to go check on Winston," Fran said. She never even sat down. She simply turned and went off to find Winston in the waiting room.

Mildred sat down in the corner chair.

It was an unpleasant room, reminiscent of a cell, only now Mildred was in the cell and the matron was the mean nurse with the hitch in her get-along. Mildred thought that she should pray for the nurse in that moment, but she didn't have any words in her. Instead, there was this desert-like interior silence that she was not supposed to like, but she did. There were times in Mildred's days and sometimes during the night too when this desert-like silence enveloped her.

When she was younger she had been scared of the purity of silence—found the emptiness of the silence startling and alarming. Now, it was a welcoming respite from the reality of her physical environment that did not come upon her very often; but when it did, she did not fight it. The interior desert seemed to offer a kind of balm that was not part of the world of day-to-day living, and in that balm there was a searching quality, a touching of this and that in her spirit. That was all. There was no edification. No illumination. Instead, there was a kind of healing consolation in being touched, being known, being allowed to exist in stillness that demanded nothing from her except the receiving of the gift of that special peace.

Fran returned to find her friend perfectly composed in the chair, her legs crossed easily at the ankles, her hands cupped, nestled in her lap, and a steady breathing that was bringing to her a fresh renewal of energy, which she needed.

Mildred smiled gently when Fran returned.

"I sent Winston home. I should have done that a long time ago. I don't know what I was thinking. He didn't need to be sitting out there. We have your car. My old boy didn't argue with me when I told him to go on home. He doesn't like hospitals," she said, the idea of more hospital time in the future lurking in the background of things she would need to think about later. She changed the subject.

Fran perched on the foot of Janie's bed. "Why is it everywhere we go the floor needs to be vacuumed?" she asked, kicking at a sliver of white paper from the straw that had been peeled.

"Everywhere I go I wish I could use their vacuum or at least use a broom," Mildred confessed.

"People don't use our kind of brooms very often anymore. They have electric broomy-things, and people use those."

"How long do you think it will take?" Mildred asked.

Almost as soon as the question was out of her mouth the Brahms lullaby began to play over the loud speaker.

"Unless there was someone else in delivery back there, that's our baby," Fran said.

"Our baby," Mildred agreed.

BABY'S BREATH

Janie was a mess.

Janie's hair was soaked and pressed away from her face. Her complexion was pale and splotchy. Like so many of their friends whom they visited from time to time in hospital rooms and nursing homes, Janie looked very small in the bed. They had changed her nightgown to a fresh one in the same pattern and style, a blue-flowered print loose-fitting tie-in-the-back hospital gown that didn't fit anyone.

"I'm thirsty," Janie said, as soon as she could speak.

"Water is in a jug over there," the nurse said, pointing. "She can have some. We will bring in the baby in a while. They're taking pictures. Doo-dah. Doo-dah," she said as she left the room.

"Not exactly Florence Nightingale," Fran remarked, pouring Janie a cup of water and jabbing a peeled straw into it.

"I detest that woman," Janie said, taking the cup. "I have asked for water before and...."

"Here you go," Fran offered, interrupting Janie's complaint. It was the smartest thing she could do for the girl who did not know yet that words of complaint helped no one and often caused the speaker to feel worse.

Janie slurped long and deeply on the glass of water and then held the blue plastic cup out to Fran to refill. Leaning her head back, she announced, "I would press some kind of charges against her if I didn't know how awful it is to have charges pressed against you, but I vowed to myself I would never knowingly do that to anyone no matter how mean. That woman shouldn't be a nurse. Or even work in a kennel. She doesn't have the love of God in her at all."

It surprised Mildred to hear Janie refer to the love of God. The idea that Janie could see that the love of God existed and, to her, was apparently missing in someone, gave Mildred a fierce and sudden hope.

"Have you seen the baby yet?" Janie asked, her voice changing. The light in her eyes did, too. "They wrapped him in a blanket. He cried."

Janie pushed herself up in bed and focused on the doorway and out into the hallway.

"Have you settled on a name?" Fran asked bravely, waiting for the answer. It took a great deal of strength to be as brave as Fran was making herself be.

Mildred looked at her oldest friend and thought: *When I grow up I want to be like you—so aware of others that I can ignore my own pain and fear and simply give as much as I can to the moment however I am needed. This is what a honeymoon can look like. This is what it sounds like when someone is in love and in trouble and still able to extend her soul to others. This is Fran Applewhite Holmes, my best friend and a follower of Jesus, the bright and morning star.*

"I put down a name on the birth certificate," Janie confessed reluctantly. "They took his footprints and put a little cap on him. It is a little blue cap. So ridiculous. You would think colors wouldn't matter anymore. But it is still blue for boys."

And then the new mother smiled suddenly. Her eyes lit up, and she made an announcement. "He is fat. I like having a fat baby. You know? People need all the strength they can get in life, and I think starting out fat is a good way to begin."

The hospital intercom played the Brahms lullaby over the loudspeaker. Not the whole piece just a few bars.

"They have been playing that song that off and on," Janie said. "It is like they can't make up their minds to play the song or not."

"They play that music every time a baby is born," Fran explained. She had taken over the conversation, and Mildred had let go.

A tear brimmed over her right eye lid and ran down her cheek. She did not want to cry, but sometimes you overflowed, tear by tear. Mildred brushed away the tear drop with her hand and pretended she had an itch.

Her head back against the pillow—her hair a sodden mess-- Janie closed her eyes and told them what she had done. "I called Little Mister, Sam, after Mr. Sam. He was good to me. Do you remember how good Mr. Sam was to me?"

Mildred nodded. "Yes, I remember Sam was good to you." Mildred's breath evened out, deepened. The need to cry eased, and the effort to stop the tears began to evaporate.

A smile as big as heaven itself filled the room and enveloped them all. People had names for this moment which happened to many people all throughout their life. Some called it the peace of God that passeth understanding. And they called it grace. But in that moment, Mildred thought of it as when Jesus smiled. *Oh, yes.*

SO LONG, ADELAIDE

Janie shifted around in the bed, trying to stretch out her legs. Her attention wandered. "Do you think his wife will mind?"

Fran answered quickly. "Oh, Sugar. Belle won't mind. A while back our old Sam was named by a local television station as Good Neighbor of the Year, but this is better."

"Sam is a great name for a little boy," Mildred approved. She wondered if they would ever call him Little Mister again. Who would even remember that for a while the Bereans' newest baby boy was known as Little Mister?

A tentative knock on the door called them all to attention.

Fran and Mildred moved toward one another automatically, preparing to be a wall between any enemy and their girl and Little Sam.

But it was only the nurse pushing Sam in a rolling baby crib. He was asleep and wrapped tightly in his blanket, his face uplifted, the skin translucent with purity and the love of God emanating from him.

"Does anyone want to see this baby?" the nurse who had just been described as not having the love of God in her asked brightly.

She sounded like a different woman altogether. *What had changed? How do you go from cold-hearted to warm-*

hearted so quickly? Maybe just pushing a baby down the hallway was enough to create this transformation.

"You can hold the little fella all you want now," the nurse suggested to Janie. "Keep his head up and his neck braced. There is no reason to be afraid. He is all yours, and he's a sweet 'un."

Janie stretched out both arms. They trembled, but her legs had settled down under the blankets. As soon as her body adjusted to all of the changes, that trembling in her arms would ease too.

Mildred wanted to tell her: *Don't be afraid of that sign of weakness. Trembles happen. They don't mean you can't go on. You will get through the trembling moments in life.*

Trembling arms outstretched, palms open, Janie waited for the nurse to find a way to place the sleeping baby on her chest. Automatically, Janie's head went down over the child, breathing in his presence, his warmth, all the hope that was born with each newborn baby. Brahms played in the background again. It was a big birthday at the hospital.

The nurse nodded to Fran and Mildred and retreated, no longer the enemy, the hateful one. She was the blessed one now, the presenter of life.

Looking up, Janie said in a tone of voice that neither woman had heard before, "Isn't he the most beautiful baby you have ever seen?"

All the women in the room nodded, a company of women who recognized the beauty of new life.

Leaning back, Baby Sam resting on her chest, Janie closed her eyes and moaned, "I need to tell the social worker."

Fran stepped forward, resolutely facing what would come next. Fran held Mildred's gaze with a clear-sighted understanding. *She is old enough to make up her own mind, and we must let her.*

"I have got a phone in my purse and her number. Do you want me to dial it for you?" Fran offered.

Janie's eyes opened slowly. She took long slow breaths, releasing the past and moving breath by breath into the present and the future that had no room for *just me alone.*

"Would you call her and say I am too tired to talk? But I have changed my mind. I have changed my mind. I don't need her." Leaning closer over the baby, Janie crooned, "We don't need her, do we? Oh, no, we don't."

Fran retrieved the business card with Adelaide's number on it, holding it to her ear. "It is ringing, but she's not picking up," she said. "It is going to voice mail," Fran explained.

Mildred walked over and wordlessly took the phone from Fran. She handed the phone to Janie and said firmly, "You need to do it. You need to say the words that need to be said. Little Sam is your baby. Adelaide is your social worker. She may not believe us. She will believe you. Tell her the truth."

"I..." Janie faltered.

Mildred shook her head, no. "If she's going to believe the message, it must come from you."

Eyes on her baby, Janie spoke clearly into the phone held near her mouth while her arms cradled her baby. "I have changed my mind. I am keeping the baby. His name is Sam, and he is mine. All mine," she said. "You don't need to

come back up here. We are all right now. Good-bye,
Adelaide."

AS TIME GOES BY

Immediately after making the call to the social worker, Fran was tired beyond words—as if she had been holding herself up until she didn't have to do that anymore, and now she allowed herself to know the truth. She was tired.

"Did I say it right?" Janie asked. "You heard me. Did I say the right words? She won't come up here, will she, because I don't want her to come up here. I don't want to see her."

"We can tell the people at the front desk not to let her in to see you."

Janie's face brightened. While she had just been through a grueling ordeal, she looked better in the eyes than she had since her release from jail. "Tell the nurse. Tell all of them that I want to be with my baby and that the social worker cannot come in."

"We will handle it," Fran assured her, fatigue taking over then. For in that moment the battle was won, and it wasn't like the Alamo. Fran's eyes met Mildred's.

Fran did not mention fatigue. Instead, she moved over to stand beside Mildred and then settled down on the arm of Mildred's chair. Her best friend oonched over, and Fran wriggled in beside her. They had sat this way many times before in other hospital rooms, but their thoughts traveled in different directions that morning.

Fran was imagining what it would be like if she were in a hospital bed recovering from a lump thing, and Mildred was wondering how she would be able to sit by herself in the chair beside Fran's hospital bed, if she were in one.

"Steev said he would baptize Little Mister when I was ready. I am not a member of the church, but Steev said—he promised—he would baptize Baby Sam. We talked about that."

"If Steev said he would do it, he will do it," Mildred confirmed, making herself come to attention.

"Steev said that babies get vaccinated and baptized. And he said it didn't matter about me not being married," she added defiantly. "Steev said babies are loved, and I am welcome to live in the loveland of Jesus. That is what Steev said, and he is a preacher. I had never heard those words before. Loveland. Loveland of Jesus."

"He is right," Fran said. "We live in the Loveland of Jesus, and here babies do get vaccinated and christened."

"He said that word, too," Janie remembered. "Do you think Steev will come back to do it today here and now? How does that work? What Steev does. What kind of water does he use? Will it be cold or warm? He said many things, and I didn't know what most of them meant."

"I think he means to christen Baby Sam later at the church in front of all the ladies, and when you are feeling like it," Fran said, immediately thinking that the boy would need a christening garment. *Would they buy one or borrow one?*

"That is right. All the Berean ladies would love to see the christening. We are going to get you home and figure out all of this as time goes by," Mildred said.

Mildred wanted to go home. She wanted to be home. She needed to check on Chase. She wanted to cook something—to tend something on the stove. Cook a roast. Cream potatoes. Eat a bowl of ice cream for dessert and watch an episode of *Everybody Loves Raymond.*

"Neither of you has to stay," Janie says. "Little Sam and I are all right now. I have got the whole hospital, and that sweet nurse looking after me. Steev is a wonderful preacher, isn't he?" Janie asked dreamily, though she had never heard him preach.

The sweet nurse. The most beautiful baby in the world. Steev is a wonderful preacher.

In Loveland, the whole world is beautiful.

"How are you feeling?" Fran asked, tenderly. Even though she was listening to the conversation, her head turned slightly toward the door. Mildred wondered if Winston had returned anyway to pick up Fran, and could Fran know that somehow just from having married him?

"Sore. Tired. All right," Janie admitted. "I am here now," she added cryptically. "I am here," she repeated to the baby, and inside those words she was introducing herself: "I am your mother, and I am here," she crooned. It was a vow. An apology for ever thinking of giving him up—for being a ringer for a while. Janie's heart was bruised with the knowledge that she had considered it.

"We will go home, freshen up, and come back later. They will want to work with you on the nursing," Fran decided, releasing Mildred to go home too. "You don't want us in the room for that."

Janie was startled. "I had forgotten that part. The nursing part. Someone told me about it once. But, there is a lot to remember." Janie looked up suddenly, her eyes searching Mildred.

"You will do fine," Mildred promised. It was the same message she said to herself in the mirror when she realized how much responsibility she felt for Janie and Little Mister and Chase.

"We will come back later," Fran promised. She walked over and placed her hand on the baby boy. Leaning over, she kissed Janie's unwashed head without flinching while Mildred went around and repeated the farewell motions.

"You will come back?" Janie asked Mildred. And her young woman's gaze searched Mildred's for some sign that she was forgiven for all of the days when she had lived behind that closed door and often slammed it

"And you will be coming home tomorrow," Mildred said.

Fran grabbed Mildred's elbow and tugged her toward the door.

In the hallway, Fran said, "And so it begins. The love affair of a new mother with her baby. And for you, Millie, you must grab any moment of rest you can find. Any spare moment is golden. For her and for you. That is how it is going to be for a while."

Fran hugged her best friend with an unrelenting grip and said, amusement in her bright blue eyes, "For an unmarried woman, your quiver is getting awfully full."

3 WEEKS LATER

The Lord upholds all who fall, and raises up all those
who are bowed down. The eyes of all look expectantly to
You, and You give them their food in due season.
You open Your hand and satisfy the desire of every
living thing.

Psalm 145: 14-16

LIVING IN LOVELAND

"Steev has offered me a job at the church."

"What kind of job?" Mildred asked carefully.

The girl had no office skills, no college. Had not graduated from high school. *Did he want her to work in the nursery?*

"Receptionist. I am going to answer the phone and take messages. Steev said he is tired of people talking into the machine. He says I have a good telephone voice. Steev said that he knows how to help me get a GED, and then maybe I could think about trade school or taking an online class. Steev said if I was working at the church, I could take an online college class and have time in between phone calls and other tasks to do my school work."

When Mildred did not answer right away, Janie added, uncomfortably, "It's not full-time. But Steev says I can bring Little Mister with me. There is a church nursery for our working mothers twice a week, and I can use that, too. Steev says the Baptist church also has a nursery during the week. Daycare. They call it Daycare. But at our church it will be free. I would have to pay the Baptists."

Mildred nodded, as if she understood. But she was slow to catch up. She had not envisioned a job for Janie.

"I don't know what people will ask me when they call the church, but Steev said that he would write me out a list of questions and answers. I can study them, and when people call and ask something, I will know what to say. Isn't that one of the smartest things you have ever heard?"

"Very intelligent," Mildred replied, wondering what kinds of questions a preacher hears to which he can write canned answers a receptionist can repeat.

"So, I will be gone during the day a lot of the time, and Mister will be, too. It will be good to have a place to go. To be. Steev says I can pick out any clothes I need from the missions' closet. Do you think I better go to church on Sunday if I am working there?"

"Probably," Mildred said.

People went to church for all kinds of reasons and working there was a good reason to start if you didn't know better.

"Steev says there is a nursery during the church services, too, and that Little Sam will be well taken care of and that I can choose a Sunday school class for people my age where I can learn what he means when he says we live in the Loveland of Jesus. Other people call it a sheepfold. I like Loveland better. In Loveland, you don't need to worry about being single and having a child."

Janie took a deep breath and said, "Steev says I will fit in."

Mildred Budge froze in place as the future of her household came into a different focus.

"I won't start work for a while. Not until Miss Fran is okay and you are okay and I am okay, and Little Mister is okay." Janie stared at Mildred, searching her for

230

reassurance that she and everyday life in Cloverdale would be okay.

"That is a good plan," Mildred approved. "And while we are planning, I am cleaning out my hope chest and wondered if you would like to have it in your room for your own things. Yours and Mister's. It would be yours to keep."

The girl did not own a single piece of furniture, and Mrs. Budge's daughter thought this girl who was moving forward in life needed a hope chest.

"Is Miss Fran going to be all right?" Janie asked quietly, as the back door opened and Belle and Sam came inside. Belle searched the room for the bassinette, found it, and went directly to Little Mister Sam.

"Do you need to hold a baby?" Janie asked Belle, as her husband Sam paced the circumference of the room, a watchman on his watch.

"I will sit there," Belle said, settling down, ignoring her husband while Janie picked up Mister and placed him in Belle's arms.

"Sam. Sam," Belle crooned.

She looked up and spoke to her husband, "This is the boy named after you, Sam. Sam. Sam."

To do honor to her husband by naming a baby after him flooded Belle with a feeling she had not experienced since her husband's diagnosis. She did not know what to call it exactly, except it was something like respect. People with dementia and the people who live with them do not get much respect even though so many of them are in so many unsung ways truly heroes. They are mostly ignored, pitied, or managed.

Belle began to rock gently, back and forth, whispering his name, "Sam. Sam." And she held the whole of life there—in her arms, against her heart, and the transcendent love of Sam's wife spread out across the room to each one of them, touching, lighting each one up, and the light of Belle's love would always be with them, each one, forever and ever. That kind of love never dies or erodes. There is no human ailment or disease that can touch it.

"I hear you," her husband said. Big Sam eyed the baby with suspicion.

Mildred could not read his mind. Neither could Belle.

"You are free to go to the other house if you like or to Miss Fran's," Janie offered. "We are all here, and we can hold down the fort."

2 8

MILDRED'S HOUSE

Her whole house was alive with the sounds of people stirring. Coming back to life.

That shouldn't be happening. Autumn was upon them. Winter was around the corner.

"Are you coming or not?" Jake called.

"Wait till you see," Chase said, his voice excited. He began to jump from one foot to the other. "The roof has solar panels."

"I have been wanting to see it," Fran said, her eyes lit up with enthusiasm. "Mildred, let's go see the playhouse."

"Are you coming or not?" Jake repeated his question.

"Mildred is behind us. She is coming with Chase. We are coming," Fran promised, stepping down from the sun porch to the ground where Jake waited for her, offering her his piano-playing hand.

Fran looked up at him, smiled, turning to find Winston, who was lingering in the kitchen where he had grown comfortable being. He hadn't always been. He was now, making himself at home wherever Fran was at home. Everyone was at home in Mildred's bungalow.

"Lead the way, Mr. Diamond. My sweetheart will be along. Mildred, too," Fran said. And though she began the short walk outdoors across the field to the playhouse, a part of Fran remained at the back door of the sunporch because Winston was inside, and she was always with him no matter where she was headed now.

Fran took mincing steps, not because her feet or legs had been hurt but because she was just a few days out of the lumpectomy. Her body was bruised, her spirit adjusting to the tempo of recovering from a setback.

"What do you think?" Jake asked as they stopped a few yards away from his retirement project.

A smile twitched at the corners of Fran's mouth. "It's charming. It is like a little fairy house out of a Disney movie. Snow White could live there. And maybe one dwarf."

"You like it?" Jake confirmed, looking behind him for Mildred.

A smile spread across Fran's face.

"It doesn't look like any playhouse I have ever seen," she marveled."

"Who said it was a playhouse?" Jake teased.

Stepping back, Fran looked up and then across. "You and the boy built this together. You and Chase."

Jake nodded. "And Sam. He was here. Belle made us peanut butter sandwiches while we worked."

Fran looked past the small playhouse to Belle's where the back door was wide open, the screen door latched to keep out flying insects. She had never known her friend to be more open, more aware, more present in the activities of others. Suddenly, Fran wanted to get to know Belle better. After all this time, there was so much to know and enjoy about her longtime friend, Belle. She was extraordinary. Sam, too, when Fran thought about him.

"Will Mildred like it?" Jake asked Mildred's best friend. He was intense. Her answer mattered to him. "Will she like it?"

Fran looked up at Jake, a good friend now and still in so many ways a stranger. He was retired and learning how to fill his days. She saw that Jake wanted to fill them with creating a good life for the friends who were becoming his adopted family. *Us,* she concluded. *All of us. And I am included, she marveled. Me? With Mildred? With Belle and Sam and Janie and Mister and everybody.*

Jake heard Fran, and nodded. "She gave me the old car," he said. "Signed it over to me without batting an eye. When I tried to tell her, it was a classic Mercedes, she did not care."

"Mildred is like that," Fran said. "And she won't even remember later, really, that she did that. You will drive it up to the house. She will see the car and wonder about it, and when you tell her it is the one she gave you from the old house, she will blink as if the memory is in there somewhere, but she won't really remember right away because that was yesterday, and Mildred lives in the day itself, every day."

He nodded. "Jesus saves. That is where our Mildred lives. What is taking her so long?" he asked, looking behind him.

She was coming slowly, at a moseying pace, her attention focused on the boy beside her who was talking, talking, telling her about the little house, and she wanted to hear every word. So many words were coming out of him now. Mildred listened carefully, storing each one of the boy's words as an answer to a morning prayer that he would come to the surface.

Belle appeared suddenly in her own back doorway. Fran saw her fidget with the small silver hook that held the screen door closed. Time passed. Sunlight fell through tree limbs. A breeze brought a memory of a childhood walk to school and the experience of the future opening up, assured but unknown, each day an adventure, each step a proclamation of trust that the Lord held the days of your life all your life long. That is what Fran knew in that moment.

Belle and Sam came out together. She was holding his arm, the way a bride does, and in a kind of way that a newly married couple moves, they came to them across the field, the light falling upon them generously. Magnificently. It was a promenade across dying grass and fallen leaves and dirt.

The sight of them walking toward the clearing in the field riveted the others. Stillness happened. Conversation ceased. The breeze continued to waft across them, bathing them in the refreshment of a changing season growing cooler but not cold yet.

And then the crunch of the newly fallen leaves and the drying grass suddenly awakened them all, and smiles of greeting happened as they all gathered together in front of the tiny house with the bark-colored exterior and the golden amber shutters.

"Are we late?" Sam asked, his voice the echo of an elder of the church who had a distant memory that people should be on time.

"Late for what?" Mildred asked, joining them at the same time. Chase was hunkering close to her, growing shy in the midst of so many people gathered in front of the small house. He grew silent, too.

"Show and tell," Belle replied. "The boys were worried about not surprising you, but I told them you would be so busy with that Momma and Baby Sam you wouldn't have time to think about this."

"Think about what?" Mildred asked, her gaze darting back toward her house. There was mounting laundry and a bottle to be warmed and a baby to be changed.

"Mildred," Jake said. "Chase wants to take you on the tour."

Chase took her hand, his gaze growing solemn and shy. He was present and eager. *Had he grown an inch?* They had an appointment to take him to the dentist. A lawyer had been called—paperwork filed to become his legal guardian.

Chase tugged for her to follow him, walking across three concrete paving stones that led up to a single step that led to the front doorway.

"Mildred Budge, why are you so slow?" Steev asked, arriving with Janie who was cradling Baby Sam.

"I am not slow at all," Mildred replied easily. "The whole world moves too fast."

"We are going this way up that step," Jake said. "Your boy helped me settle that step there. We are going to add another one, but that is the big step up for today."

Mildred saw the challenging step, saw the black wrought iron handrail. "It is a mighty fancy playhouse," she remarked, imagining a community library where everyone could leave their books and then borrow what they wanted.

The idea delighted her. Maybe she would become a librarian after all. Her mother in heaven would smile to see her daughter arranging books to loan on shelves and nearby neighbors coming back to thumb through them, to choose one for company later before bedtime. A little neighborhood library where people could drop off books and take what they wanted.

Mildred had stopped moving—just stopped. It was a wonderful moment, an ordinary extraordinary moment, a glorious moment, the kind of moment you experience when you take the time to notice it. She wanted to find Fran, see Fran, and smile and nod. *Isn't this a perfect moment? We are all here together.*

"We are going to add another step, so it is kind of a big step right now. But you can do it."

"Of course, I can do it," Mildred said. She hoped there would be bookshelves inside and maybe a water cooler one day.

Jake waited for Fran to follow Mildred up, and it was harder for her. There was a moment when Fran was lifting her foot, and she stopped as if she were thinking, *am I going to go on? Am I?* After a flicker of hesitation, Fran stepped up and landed beside Mildred. Jake waited for Winston to go next—to stand beside Fran. Belle and Sam crowded in behind them, filling in the space of the single room of the tiny house. Steev and Janie waited outside with Little Mister.

"There is a light switch," Jake said, reaching around Mildred to the wall behind her shoulder.

His hand flicked the switch.

And just like that the small room lit up.

Mildred couldn't figure out what she was seeing at first. And then the shapes began to make sense. There were no book shelves, though. No water cooler. It was a strange space—not like anything she had seen before.

Chase moved around the small area, pointing out the features. Every time she followed where his hand was pointing, he waited for her to smile. She did. And every time she smiled, Chase smiled, his eyes pure and lit with expectation that she would be pleased.

There was small sink—a foot of counter space.

A small countertop stove with two burners.

A small bathroom with a beige accordion door.

"There's even a shower, about the size they have on a submarine," Jake said.

The narrow space reminded Mildred of an old-fashioned elevator she had ridden in as a girl in that old, old church building downtown on Catoma Street where a lone man pushed and pulled open the accordion door to take a lone passenger at a time up and down from the Sunday school rooms in the basement to the sanctuary for the church service. She thought of him in that moment and the way it felt to go up and down, and she wished she could remember his name. A great kindness had emanated from him, and sometimes he would take her up and down several times after Sunday school and before the church service began because she liked to feel the elevator bump when it landed. *You're going places*, he had told the little girl more than once, pushing back the accordion door to let her pass through when it was finally time to leave, and she had believed him. Thinking of him in that moment, she believed he was right, for though she had not traveled far she had lived in many dimensions—gone to many places in her soul, and they were real.

A small coffeemaker hung underneath a small cabinet with two doors.

Jake reached up and showed her the contents. "Belle has been stocking these for us. She knows what you like. Tomato bisque soup. Oatmeal. Instant grits. A small can of Maxwell House coffee, original recipe."

"I like all of that," Mildred acknowledged quietly. She wasn't understanding what she was seeing. This wasn't a child's playhouse.

"There a little refrigerator, and it has a small freezer. Chase chose what goes in there."

"Banana popsicles," she acknowledged, opening the freezer door. "And fudgesicles."

"He said you would like both of those."

"I like bananas and fudgesicles," she concurred. "Perhaps you will share them with me," Mildred said, her gaze fixed on the small boy whose face was alive, keen with excitement and sharing.

There was a small narrow bench beneath a square window. And there was a chair in front of a fold-up table with two legs. It was lowered down, balanced on those two legs, holding up a coffee cup filled with writing pens, and beside it, three new Steno pads.

"This is where you can write your Sunday school lessons. Your meditations. Maybe you will write a book. People do that now. We didn't put a Bible here because we know you have your own, but we got you a stack of those steno pads you like from Walgreens, and there is a cupful of pens," Jake said. "You are a Sunday school teacher, and you need a place to write your lessons."

Mildred had given her lesson on *When Jesus Smiled,* the Sunday before. She had been so excited about it. Standing in front of her Berean sisters, her voice had quavered though. It had taken her through the opening prayer and the first hymn to get her voice back to normal.

Then, one of the Berean sisters had fainted. Two deacons had been summoned with a wheelchair and escorted her to the back door where a family member would collect her and take her home.

Mildred's lesson about Jesus smiling had been interrupted by the trembles of life that happened all the time to everyone and certainly to the Bereans. By the time the class turned its attention back to the list of Bible passages where they could see Jesus smiling if they looked, everyone was discomfited not only with their classmate's problem but with the imagined idea that she could be next to teeter, be put in a wheel chair, and rolled to the back door to be collected by someone and taken somewhere.

Mildred had gotten through the verses, asked for prayer requests, and they had spent the rest of the class time praying for others. No one had seemed to see Jesus smile. They only saw him weep. But Jesus smiled. Oh, yes. She resolved to try and give the lesson another day, another way.

"And the whole place will run on solar energy," Jake explained. "We haven't put all the panels we need on the roof yet, but they're coming."

"You have done too much," she said automatically.

"Not if you like it," he replied firmly. "You needed a room of your own, and that is what you are getting today. You needed room to write your Sunday school lessons."

"Or meditations," Fran interjected.

Jake nodded. "That is right."

And then he changed the subject abruptly, peering through the porthole of a window.

"What would you think about having a well dug? There is a growing concern nationwide about the supply of water, and I am pretty sure Sam and Chase and I could tap into something out here. Our own access to water could come in handy one day."

Mildred didn't answer Jake in that moment. She heard Jake, but the question would arise slowly in her consciousness later when he brought the subject up again. Jake didn't mind the pace at which Mildred lived her life. He was learning that Mildred responded slowly, thoughtfully, carefully, but she eventually reacted to what she had heard. She wasn't ignoring you.

"It is a tiny house," Mildred said finally. "It is not a playhouse. It is a tiny house. They have them on television."

"It is your tiny house. Or your writing room. Or a playhouse. Call it anything you like."

She thought of early morning. She thought of the quiet and the distance from that back door of her bungalow to this quiet space with a different view. She was ready for a different view. Here, she could see Steev's house and the street from a different angle and a portion of Belle's and Sam's house through the front window. And she could see more sky, more trees, too.

"I can be here," she affirmed. "I can be here," she repeated.

Chase snuggled closer to Mildred, tilting in against her. Fran and Winston held hands, Fran leaned against her husband, not ready to say that she needed to go home. *Not yet. She was still a go-getter. Yes, she was. There was chemo and radiation to come, but she was a go-getter.*

Belle watched as Sam grabbed one of Mildred's bananas, peeled it, and began to eat. "Why so quiet, Millie Boo?"

"I am thinking," she said.

"Danger, danger," Sam said, eating his banana.

"We don't need to move," Mildred concluded, with awe.

Jake nodded.

"Thank you. Thank you," she repeated. "Thank you, everybody," she said as a lesson about Solomon rose up in her, for she was very interested in teaching young people that while David's son was reported to be the wisest man of his time, being smart wasn't enough. *Oh, no.* Being wise had not stopped Solomon from failing. And if she wrote a Sunday school lesson about Solomon, she wanted to write another one about his daddy, too. Oh, the story of David should be told from a church lady's perspective. She could just see that young man with his sling shot facing down the enemy and in doing it teaching the people who came after him how to face an enemy with the tools you owned and fight. Church ladies face enemies differently, but they do fight.

Oh, the stories of the Bible were electrifying, soul-filling, energizing words that helped every person who read them live a better life. *Oh, yes.*

"You tell me when you are ready, and I will put out that For Sale or For Rent sign in front of the other house," Jake offered.

"We can all just stay right here," she concluded. "We can all live right here," she said.

Delight suffused the perfect moment, flooding the small house. Everyone was smiling.

"That's right," Jake agreed. "Stay right where you and Chase and Janie and Mister belong here in the heart of Cloverdale."

BONUS CONTENT: MISS BUDGE GOES TO FOUNTAIN CITY

A CHRISTMAS STORY

Mildred Budge had not always been a gambler.

But after she went into business with her friend Fran Applewhite, it had become partially her responsibility to restock their inventory over at the two antique booths in the local Emporium. When Mildred couldn't find anything to buy at the early morning estate sale, she had to choose something because she couldn't go home empty-handed.

So, the devout church lady gambled on a mystery box. There was no instinct in her that prompted the purchase. The moment didn't feel lucky. God didn't tell her to buy it.

Mildred Budge bought the mystery box because it had a plastic handle on the top that felt like it would hold together long enough for her to carry to the car, and the box was priced at the amount of money she had in the side pocket of her purple corduroy pants: ten dollars.

"Here you go," Mildred said to the unshaven, sleepy college boy wearing a yellow T-shirt with the incongruous words on the front: Estate Sales R Us.

The company specialized in helping relatives clean out the houses of the recently deceased, doing all the work for a nifty 30% of the gross receipts for the day.

After handing over her money, Mildred walked through the house toward the front door without pausing to examine any of the vintage keepsake holiday ornaments on the Christmas tree in the foyer. The ornaments were also on sale.

Mildred caught a glimpse of Elvis Presley in a startling white outfit with bell bottom pants ostensibly having just sung *Blue Christmas*, a duo of chipmunks wearing Santa hats waving silver icicles like swords, Betty Boop in a fur-lined red outfit blowing a kiss, and all kinds of reindeer in different sizes and prices that sparkled with glitter.

Some reindeer were playful and Rudolphish. Other reindeer were stately and august. Mildred Budge had an affection for reindeer that she did not actively cultivate, but when she saw Prancer, the retired fifth-grade school teacher smiled with longing. She loved Prancer!

But seeing Prancer was enough.

Mildred Budge didn't need to own a reindeer ornament. She could enjoy seeing Prancer and walk right on by; so, she did, lugging the mystery box which had grown heavy fast.

Mildred walked back to her car, positioning the prize box in the back seat and stopping only briefly to inhale the sharp winter air.

Someone nearby had a kitchen window cracked and was frying bacon for breakfast. A door slammed loudly, and a woman called out, "Honey, come on inside. Breakfast is ready."

"She is the one frying bacon," Mildred whispered to God. "And I am going home and make some for myself."

Mildred had eaten only one slice of toast with the last teaspoon of homemade pear preserves that one of her Sunday school chums had given her—it was barely enough to cover the toast! — and she had sipped a fast cup of strong coffee. As a consequence of that meager repast, Mildred Budge was hungry.

Shoppers had to hit estate sales early if they were going to get the best bargains, and she had been up since 5 Am in order to get to it by 7:15, which was her arrival time. That fifteen minutes past the starting hour of the estate sale had cost her some of the best deals. The other vendors had gotten there at 6:30 and powered through, making fast decisions and handing over their dollars with the kind of assurance Mildred did not feel when she made a purchase.

Still, Fran's business partner had snagged a mystery box. And now with that well-taped cardboard box safely procured to fulfill her obligation to find some items to replenish their always dwindling inventory, Mildred was going home and cook a proper breakfast and then practice her Christmas carols on her old Baldwin studio piano for the Bereans, the members of her long-time Sunday school class. The girls expected her to get them in the holiday spirit by helping them sing the carols of the season.

'First, a proper breakfast, and then I shall practice the carols so that my hands won't shake on Sunday morning,' Mildred resolved.

That was the plan.

Miss Budge Goes to Fountain City, a Christmas story, is available now on Amazon.

Check it out and other titles released through Quotidian Books.

BOOKS BY DAPHNE SIMPKINS

The Mildred Budge Novels
Mildred Budge in Cloverdale Book 1
Mildred Budge in Embankment Book 2
The Bride's Room Book 3
Kingdom Come Book 4

The Short Adventures of Mildred Budge
Miss Budge in Love Book 1
The Mission of Mildred Budge Book 2
Miss Budge Goes to Fountain City Book 3

The Mildred Budge Friendship Stories
Belle: A Mildred Budge Friendship Story

Stand-alone novels
Lovejoy a novel about desire
Christmas in Fountain City

Memoirs and essays
The Long Good Night
A Cookbook for Katie
What Al Left Behind
Blessed

What Makes a Man a Hero?

Other
11 DIY Small Talks

ABOUT DAPHNE SIMPKINS

Daphne is an Alabama writer best known for her Mildred Budge series. But she has written frequently about family life in the South and caregiving.

To sign up for news about Mildred Budge and other releases from Quotidian Books, visit the website www.DaphneSimpkins.org

Daphne Simpkins

Contact Daphne through her website www.DaphneSimpkins.org.
Or follow her on Amazon, Goodreads, and BookBub.

Made in the USA
Monee, IL
21 September 2023

43125189R00144